P9-CMX-101

THE
BEST WORST
THING

Peachtree

LITTLE, BROWN AND COMPANY
New York • Boston

This book is a work of fiction. Names, characters, places, and incidents are the product of the author's imagination or are used fictitiously. Any resemblance to actual events, locales, or persons, living or dead, is coincidental.

Copyright © 2016 by Kathleen Lane

All rights reserved. In accordance with the U.S. Copyright Act of 1976, the scanning, uploading, and electronic sharing of any part of this book without the permission of the publisher is unlawful piracy and theft of the author's intellectual property. If you would like to use material from the book (other than for review purposes), prior written permission must be obtained by contacting the publisher at permissions@hbgusa.com. Thank you for your support of the author's rights.

Little, Brown and Company

Hachette Book Group
1290 Avenue of the Americas, New York, NY 10104
Visit us at lb-kids.com

Little, Brown and Company is a division of Hachette Book Group, Inc.
The Little, Brown name and logo are trademarks of Hachette Book Group, Inc.

The publisher is not responsible for websites (or their content) that are not owned by the publisher.

First Edition: June 2016

Library of Congress Cataloging-in-Publication Data

Lane, Kathleen, 1967–
The Best Worst Thing / by Kathleen Lane.—First edition.
pages cm
Summary: "Maggie sees injustice and danger everywhere, and she does not like it one bit, so she devises intricate ways of controlling her own world, and a larger, more dangerous plan for protecting everyone else"—Provided by publisher.
ISBN 978-0-316-25781-7 (hardcover)—ISBN 978-0-316-25783-1 (ebook)—ISBN 978-0-316-25780-0 (library edition ebook) [1. Safety—Fiction.] I. Title.
PZ7.L2501Pr 2016
[Fic]—dc23

2015012906

10 9 8 7 6 5 4 3 2 1

RRD-C

Printed in the United States of America

For Mom, Dad, Cristianne, and Joan

It's the night we're going to get murdered so we're sleeping on the living room floor.

Me and my sisters, Mom and Dad, all of us on the floor in front of the couch we pushed up against the wall to make room for our sleeping bags.

The murderer is walking around our neighborhood. He's walking down our street. He's down by the duck pond, hiding under the weeping willow. He's sneaking through the Dugans' yard, creeping through the Cooneys' grapes, coming to get us.

"He'll probably try to come right through that window there," Dad says, and Polly and I scream the screams Dad calls our bee-sting screams and slide our sleeping bags away from the window, as far away as we can get, until we're pushed into the couch pushed against the wall.

"Bill, stop," Mom says, "you're scaring them."

Dad was still at work when we saw it on TV, on the news that we weren't supposed to be watching because Polly's too little, but Mom went to answer the phone during *Odd Squad* and she was on the phone for a long time. After *Odd Squad* it was *Judge Judy* and after *Judge Judy* it was yellow tape around the Mini Mart. It was a body shape under a sheet. In the corner of the screen there was a picture of a man with a fat chin and his hair pulled back in a ponytail.

"What's *suspect at large* mean?" I asked.

"It means he's large, stupid," Tana said.

I didn't hear everything the newsman said because of Tana talking and Polly coughing, but I did hear *shot and killed,* I heard *fled on foot.* I heard *Elm Avenue* and my brain started singing the address song, the one Mom used to make us sing on the way to school. *My name is Maggie Alder and this is where I li-ive, 845, 845, 845 Elm Av-e-nue.* She turned it into a song so we could sing it to police if we got lost. So we could sing it to the fire department if we had to call 9-1-1. 9-1-1's another song she taught us. *9-1-2, that won't do. 9-1-1, let's see that thumb,* and we were three thumbs-up in Mom's rearview mirror.

Elm Avenue, fled on foot. I was still working it out in my head when Tana started yelling, "He's on our street!" which made me and Polly start yelling, "He's on our street! He's on our street!" Then we were running our yells and into the kitchen. Then Mom was yelling, yelling at us for yelling. "I thought your arm got cut off!" she yelled. I don't know whose arm she meant, whose arm she was so worried about getting cut off, Polly's arm or Tana's arm, I hope my arm.

"Some guy shot the checkout lady!" Tana yelled. "At the Mini Mart! We were *just* there, we were there like three hours ago!" As soon as she said that, it was like I was back at the Mini Mart. It was like I could see the lady behind the counter laughing and saying, "You girls having some lunch?" while she was ringing up our candy. It was like all that licorice I ate turned into a big red snake twisting around in my stomach and I had to squeeze my eyes shut so I wouldn't see her get shot.

"Maybe we saw him!" Tana said. It kind of seemed like she was happy about it, like the time she saw Katy Perry in the grocery store, even though I don't really think she saw Katy Perry, because why would Katy Perry just be hanging out in Albertsons buying cheese puffs!

Mom said, "Oh God" and "Oh how awful." I saw her look out the window into the backyard even though she said she didn't, even though she said, "No, I think he's in jail" when I asked if she thought the murderer was in our backyard. "Oh great," Tana said like she always says when I'm worried about something or Polly's crying.

When Dad got home, Polly and I yelled, "Lock the

door! Lock the door!" We made him go all around the house checking the windows and under the beds and inside the closets. I yelled for Dad to look behind the dresser and Polly yelled for Dad to look inside our pajama drawer, and that's when Mom said, "Well, I guess we're all sleeping together tonight." Dad said, "All of us in one bed?" and that's how Mom came up with the idea of sleeping bags. "It'll be like camping," she said.

Mom went downstairs to make us some dinner but Polly and I made Dad stand in our room while we got our sleeping bags out of our closet, while we got our pajamas out of our drawers and ran to our beds for pillows. "You're being such a baby," Tana said when I asked Dad to walk us downstairs, even though I only asked because Polly didn't want to go down without him. "I can't believe you're starting middle school in like *two* days!"

Tana left without us and Dad said he had to shower. "Come on now," he said when Polly and I wouldn't let go of his arms, "you have each other." So we got our soft stabbing parts all wrapped up in our sleep things and each other. We threw our sleeping bags down the stairs and ran like the murderer was chasing us to the bottom.

Tana was sitting at the kitchen table looking through a magazine, Mom was making us a living room picnic. We wrapped our arms around her while she stuck roast beef on bread and opened up a jar of mayonnaise. We followed her to the napkin drawer to get the napkins. We followed her into the living room to put the plate of sandwiches on the coffee table, then back into the kitchen where we squeezed up around her while she poured us some Cokes. We were a six-legged creature walking to the freezer for ice.

In the living room Polly and I sit cross-legged inside our sleeping bags and bunch them all around us until only our heads are sticking out and sometimes an arm when we need a bite of sandwich. Tana's pretending to read her magazine. I know she's pretending because she hasn't flipped a page in forever. I wish our living room window wasn't so big. I wish it wasn't so black.

"This is fun," Mom says. "We should do this more often."

"Too bad we don't get many murderers around these parts." Dad's all done with his shower, he's wearing his striped pajamas that look like one of his work shirts stretched over his whole body. He sits down in the La-Z-Boy near the big window, too close to the big window. The murderer sees Dad. The murderer shoots Dad right through the window. The window is breaking, Dad is dead. Please don't let the murderer shoot Dad, please don't let the murderer shoot Dad, I say with sleeping bag over my mouth so no one will hear, and twice to make it even.

When the neighbor's dog starts barking, Polly starts

crying, so Mom sits on the couch behind us and pats Polly through her sleeping-bag puff. She says, "It's probably just another dog."

"I'll go have a look around," Dad says.

"Don't be—!" Tana yells. (I think she almost said *stupid*!) "He has a gun!"

"He has a gun!" Polly and I yell.

Dad grabs the mustard knife off the sandwich plate and makes a bad-guy look that's supposed to be funny, but it isn't funny because our dad, I just now for the first time realized, is a small man. Our dad is a very small man and he has skinny arms. He has skinny arms because he's old, he's much older than our friends' dads. He doesn't wear baseball hats, he doesn't drive a truck. Our dad wears button shirts and sells insurance and carves sea animals out of driftwood.

Now he's doing his pretend tough cowboy walk into the kitchen. We hear the back door open and close but there aren't any locking sounds, Dad didn't lock us in, he just left the back door open for the murderer.

Someone just coughed! Outside! Now my heart is coughing, *ka-ka ka-ka* in my chest. I don't know if it was Dad coughing or the murderer coughing, or maybe the murderer just heard Dad cough and now he's going to shoot him! Please don't let the murderer shoot Dad, please don't let the murderer shoot Dad.

"He's just looking around," Mom says. She says it again,

even though we didn't ask, even though we know she can't see him out there in the dark.

"Are you worried? About Dad?" I know she's worried, I can tell from her voice.

"Oh great," Tana says, and Mom says, "Maggie, please. He's just looking around." Polly pulls her sleeping bag around her face until she's just a nose. "Don't worry," I whisper to her nose, "he's just looking around."

But why is he taking so long!

He's taking so long because he's *dead*. He's under a sheet with his face covered up. Our yard is wrapped in yellow tape. The suspect is large.

When the kitchen door opens, we are so fast out of our sleeping bags and on top of Mom, even Tana dives on Mom, only there isn't enough Mom for all our arms and legs and now the murderer is stomping through the kitchen, the murderer is coming to get us. I can tell Tana's praying even though I can't hear her. I can see her chin moving, and Tana praying means Tana's scared, and Tana scared means we're all going to die!

"Don't be scared," I whisper to Polly, "it's just Dad. It's just Dad, don't be scared. It's just Dad."

I don't let go, I don't even open my eyes, not even when Mom yells, "What on earth took you so long!" I keep holding on, I don't want to look, because what if the murderer shot Dad, what if Dad's all bloody, what if the murderer followed

Dad into the house and now he's going to shoot us too! Please don't let the murderer shoot us, please don't let the murderer shoot us.

I don't let go until I hear his voice. "Chased him all the way to China," he says, and we leap off Mom and onto Dad. Tana's just standing there but Polly's hugging Dad's stomach and I'm hugging Dad's neck. I have to kiss his cheeks, I have to give them two kisses each so the murderer won't come back and get us while we're sleeping, but I can only reach one cheek and now Dad's saying, "Okay, girls," and unwrapping our arms. I have to do it, I have to kiss his other cheek!

"Maggie," Dad says when I grab his head. I don't like the way he said *Maggie,* he said it kind of mean, but at least I kissed both his cheeks, so now we can all go to sleep and nothing bad will happen.

We're not dead.

We're eating our Cocoa Puffs, Mom's making herself a slim shake.

Wait. "What about Dad?"

"He's fine," Mom says, "he's just at work."

"Are you sure? How do you know? Did he call you?"

"Oh great."

I wish Tana wouldn't say *Oh great* after every single thing I say! It's not like I *want* to be worried about Dad!

Mom says yes, even though I know it's not true, Dad didn't call her, Dad never calls her.

"Did they catch the guy?" Tana asks.

I didn't think about that! What if they didn't catch him! What if he's still running around shooting people! And why does Tana get to ask about the murderer and I don't get to ask about Dad? *Oh great*, I say, but only in my head. Next time I'm going to yell it!

"Maybe he's hiding in the bushes," Polly whispers. She's twisting her hair how she does before she puts it in her mouth.

"I guarantee you he is not hiding in our bushes," Mom says. "We'd have heard him hollering." She means from all the branches scratching him up. She means me last year when I went into the bushes looking for Polly's yellow pony.

"SlimFast should be called SlimSlow," Mom says. "But I did read somewhere that muscle weighs more than fat so maybe I'm just getting stronger." She winks at us so we know it's okay to laugh. Mom doesn't always think fat's funny.

"Can I have some?" Tana says.

It's the pink flavor, the Strawberry Supreme.

"Me too?"

"Me too?"

"You girls eat your breakfast," Mom says, so we do, but we want the SlimSlow, we want to lick the Strawberry Supreme off our lips.

There are only seven puffs left in my bowl. I need one more puff to make it even.

"You can't have the prize!" Tana yells. She tries to grab the box away but I make my hand big inside so she can't get it off my arm.

"I'm not getting the prize! I'm getting a puff!"

"Maggie," Mom says, "don't stick your hand in there, pour them out," so I pour and hope for even.

Mom sits down with us and we watch the pink go up and down her straw. Polly watches with her tongue out. Polly's tongue is always out. Unless she's eating. Unless she's talking.

"I want to lose weight too," Tana says.

"Oh no you don't. Don't you even say that. You girls are perfect just the way you are."

"So are you!" I say.

"So are you!" Polly says.

"Well," Mom says. She holds her hair clip between her lips and pulls her hair back behind her neck, getting it all neat and straight, but she always leaves some out, I feel bad for the hairs that get left out. It's the clip with the green stones, the one she got in Mexico before we were born.

"Tell us the story," Polly says. Probably it's the clip that made her think of it. Sometimes it's watermelon and sometimes it's driftwood. Sometimes it's the *hungry for your touch* song. They're all part of the story of Mom meeting Dad, and Mom and Dad falling in love and making us. *Then came you three*, that's how the story ends. *Of course, we were too young to know anything* is somewhere in the middle. I don't really know what that means but she says it every time.

"Let's see," Mom says with her lips still holding the clip. Her lips didn't move at all, not even a little bit. "Let's see," I whisper, trying to keep my lips still too. "Let's see," I whisper again.

When her hair's ready, she holds it together with one hand and takes her clip out of her mouth with the other. Polly and I get out of our chairs and stand behind her so we can see how she does it. She does it without looking, her fingers know how to do it all on their own. Polly pretends she has a clip and gathers her hair together. I do it too, even though I have short hair so it takes more pretending.

"Your dad was walking up the beach with his friends."

"And there you were," Polly says.

"There I was."

"Pretty as a piece of driftwood," I say.

"Well, that's what your dad said. Didn't sound like much of a compliment to me, but that was before I knew about your dad and his whittling."

"Carving," Tana says, because Dad doesn't like whittling. Dad says whittling is like thumb twiddling.

"Carving." The way Mom says it, we know the story's over. Mom doesn't always finish the story.

I don't want to go outside because of the murderer but Mom says it's going to rain later so we should get out there and run around. Also it's the last day of summer, which I wish she wouldn't have reminded me because tomorrow I have to go to middle school and I really really *really* don't want to.

"That man is long gone," Mom says. "He's probably halfway to Arkansas by now."

I see Ms. Olsen's map of America. I see the pork chop with the colored squares. The murderer is running over the squares on his way to Arkansas. He runs over Arkansas and Tennessee and I can't remember what comes next, and over Alabama and Florida and right into the ocean. "Help me! Help me!" he yells, so a sailor throws him a rope and pulls him onto the boat. Then the murderer gets his gun out of his pocket and shoots the sailor in the heart.

Tana won't let us hold on to her so Polly and I hold on to each other. The murderer is everywhere. He's behind the garage, he's behind that tree. He's up on the roof aiming his gun at our heads. Please don't let the murderer shoot our heads, please don't let the murderer shoot our heads.

When Gordy Morgan's dog barks, Polly and I scream, we say that dog gave us heart attacks. I don't like that dog. He has one blue eye and one white eye, he looks like a wolf, and one time when Gordy was taking him for a walk he started barking at us and Gordy said, "Good dog." He said, "Should I let you off your leash so you can eat up those girls?" and all the time we were running home, Gordy's dog was eating me up, eating up my arms and my legs, chewing up my ears.

At first I thought that was Gordy coughing but it was only Mr. Gullick. Mr. Gullick lives on the other side of the fence, behind our house, and right next to Mr. Gullick is where Gordy and his dog live. I like when Mr. Gullick's outside because he can protect us from Gordy and now he can protect us from the murderer too.

There's a hole in the fence between our yards and if we hold our eyes real still we can see Mr. Gullick's rabbits. If you push your face against the wood you can see inside two of the cages, but we know there are more because one time Dad left the wheelbarrow out, the one he used to push us around the yard in before we got too big, and we stood on top of it. I could only get my nose up on the fence so all I saw was grass, and all Polly could see was sky, but Tana told us Mr. Gullick has like six cages, all in a row, and a table with a knife on it, probably for chopping up food for his rabbits. I wish we had a ladder in the garage. I wish there were more holes in Mr. Gullick's fence! I don't know why he needs such a tall fence anyway. Tana said it's for keeping dogs out, but you don't need a fence that high to keep out dogs.

Sometimes when we look through the hole we see Mr. Gullick's big old belly. He wears these tight white undershirts that are kind of see-through so you can see his belly hair underneath, all smashed into swirls like how Polly draws smoke blowing out a chimney. One time Tana said that he looked pregnant, like he could have a baby any second now, which is kind of true and kind of funny, especially when she said *a hairy baby*, but kind of mean too.

Tana's hogging the hole again, she's always hogging the hole. "Awww," she says, "they're snuggling."

"Let me see!"

"Stop pushing! You're going to give me splinters!"

Polly says, "I want to see too."

It's all true, all our yelling and pushing, but it's also part of us making the girl sounds that sometimes make Mr. Gullick say, *You girls want to hold one?*

"Awwwwww," I say when Tana finally lets me have a turn at looking.

"This one here's about three months old." When I look up, Mr. Gullick's big hairy hand is hanging over the fence and there's fur sticking out between his fingers.

I get to hold her first. She's a little white bunny, the sweetest little bunny, the softest little bunny. "Aw, she's so cute!"

Polly's petting bunny's head with her finger and Tana keeps saying, "My turn! My turn!" and trying to grab her away.

"I just got her! She's shaking, she's scared." I can feel her heart thumping under my finger. More like humming than thumping. Like how your throat feels when you hum, when you put your fingers on your throat and hum.

"You girls keep her over there a minute while I get this cage cleaned."

In the grass, we sit shoe to shoe. We make our legs into fences. I pick some grass and hold it out for bunny. Tana makes kissing sounds and Polly whispers, "Come here little rabbit, come here little bunny bunny."

"What's her name, Mr. Gullick?" Tana hollers at the fence.

Mr. Gullick never names his rabbits but we keep asking anyway because one time his grandkid named one of them Jesus and we thought that was so funny. Jesus the rabbit!

"Doesn't have a name," Mr. Gullick hollers back.

I name her Snow Cone and Tana names her Cloudy and Polly names her Cloudy too, so Tana changes her name to Sugar and we all say, "Sugar! Sweet sugar, sweet sweet sugar. Here Sugar, here girl."

We play with Sugar until Mr. Gullick says, "Okay now, let's have her back," then we all three pick her up, we all three carry her back over to the fence. We are six hands holding her up in the sky for Mr. Gullick.

When our hands are empty we count how many hairs stuck onto our skin. Tana has four and Polly has three and I have five. I look in the grass for another hair so I'll have six but I don't see any.

"What are you doing?" Tana says. "Maggie's looking for rabbit poop!"

"Here," Polly says, "you can have one of mine." She picks a hair off one of her fingers and sticks it onto the back of my hand so now I have even.

I get the biggest piece.

It's my favorite, chocolate with chocolate frosting. "That's a ton!" It's like two pieces of cake. Dad's at work so he isn't here to say it's too much.

"It's our first day too!" Tana says, but I'm the only one starting a new school tomorrow. Tana has to wait two years to get the biggest piece. Polly has to wait three.

"You are going to love middle school," Mom says.

"No she isn't! She's going to hate it!"

"Tana's just trying to make you nervous," Mom says, and gives Tana a *watch it* look.

I know Tana's right, I know I'm going to hate it. Tana says you only have four minutes between classes so I better not get lost and I better not forget my locker combination, but I can't even practice my locker combination because we don't get our numbers until tomorrow!

"Kelsey and Hailey will be there," Mom says, "and all your other friends."

Frosting comes out of Tana's mouth when she laughs. It looks like mud. I don't have any other friends, I know that's why Tana's laughing. Not really, not good friends.

"Polly, you look like you're the one starting middle school!" Mom says, and pulls Polly's hair back like she's making her a ponytail.

It's true, Polly looks scared. I'm holding my scared in so Tana won't know, but everyone knows when Polly's scared because she chews on her hair—even though Mom got her the special shampoo that tastes bad. Now she's laughing, though. Now we're all laughing, thinking about Polly already being scared about middle school, which makes me feel a little less scared, but only for a minute because as soon as we're done laughing all the scared comes back. It's like a balloon filling up my stomach, bigger and bigger, and I am trying so hard right now not to cry.

Front door locked, kitchen door locked, kitchen window closed, basement door closed.

"Maggie, I already locked all the doors," Mom says, but what if she forgot one? Wait, I can't remember if I checked the kitchen door.

Kitchen door locked. Living room windows closed, sliding glass door locked. Nobody behind the bathroom door, nobody hiding behind the shower curtain, bathroom window closed. It's safe to brush my teeth now, the murderer won't grab my neck while I'm spitting out my toothpaste.

Nobody behind our bedroom door. Nobody in the closet. Nobody under mine and Polly's bunks, nobody under Tana's bed. Bedroom window closed.

Please don't let the murderer kill us, please don't let the

murderer kill us. Please let middle school be good, please let middle school be good.

"Are you going to do that every single night?"

"Do what?"

"I saw you looking under our beds."

I probably am going to do it every single night but I don't want to tell Tana that or she'll beg Mom for her own room again, even though there isn't another room for her, unless she wants to sleep in Dad's carving room. I would be too scared to sleep alone in that room with all those seals and sea lions. I bet at night it would feel like you're in the ocean, way down in the deep dark water just waiting for a shark to come eat you.

I didn't sleep last night, NOT EVEN FOR ONE MINUTE.

I was too worried about middle school. I was too worried about the murderer. I think I dreamed that the murderer was my teacher! Now I'm super tired and I'll probably get lost. I'm already lost, I have no idea where my homeroom is! I can't find my paper that says where my homeroom is!

"Oh great," Tana says because Mom said she had to walk me to my first class. Her lips are covered in that pink lip gloss that makes them stick together a little when she talks.

"I found it!" It was in the front pocket of my backpack. This backpack has too many pockets. "25A."

The hall is so long! It's like a road, it's like a tunnel. It's loud and crowded and it makes my eyes sting. One, two, one, two, one, two, one, two, one, two—

"Maggie!" Tana says because I went too far, I walked past 25A.

One, two, one—

"Are you counting again?"

"No."

"Yes you were, I heard you."

"Two," I whisper while Tana's saying hi to some boy. I have no idea who that boy is.

Tana says she'll meet me here after school. She says, "I hope you have a nice day," but I bet she only said that because Mom told her to.

Kelsey is already sitting at a desk. She takes her notebook off the desk next to her. "I saved you a seat." Hailey isn't here because Hailey has a different homeroom teacher.

"We should have worn jeans," Kelsey whispers. "We're the only ones in the whole class wearing skirts." Kelsey's wearing a green skirt I've never seen before and boots I've never seen before. She says, "At least you have leggings under yours."

I only wore leggings because Tana said I better if I didn't want to look dumb. Kelsey doesn't have a big sister to tell her how to be. "That girl's wearing a skirt," I say.

"But she's fat!"

I kind of know what Kelsey means but I still think it

wasn't a very nice thing to say. I hope that girl didn't hear her. Also, Kelsey didn't have to say *fat*. You can say *heavy*. You can say *a little on the heavy side*.

Our teacher has short gray hair and a little bit of a mustache. "Class, when the bell rings you should already be settled in your seats. If you are not settled when the bell rings, you will be marked as late." She points to a piece of paper taped to the whiteboard: 3 LATES = 1 ABSENCE. I don't think I'm going to like Ms. Morris. But she just smiled and said, "Welcome to middle school," so maybe she's nice? It's hard to tell.

Now she's walking around the room putting little pieces of paper on our desks. They look like fortune cookie fortunes but they aren't fortunes, they're our locker combinations. Mine is not a fortune at all! It's like the opposite of a fortune, two evens and an odd. But there are three numbers, which is another odd so that's two odds, which makes even, so I guess it's okay.

"Did you get a good number?" I ask Kelsey but Kelsey isn't looking at her combination, she's looking around the room.

"I am totally wearing jeans tomorrow," she says.

At lunchtime, all the girls from Riverside Elementary are sitting at the same cafeteria table. We all agree that the Jell-O here is much better than the Jell-O at Riverside, it's softer, but we don't like one of the lunch ladies. She was mean to Josie because Josie couldn't remember what the brown stuff was called and when she said she wanted the brown stuff, the lunch lady said *sloppy joes* in a really mean voice that made Josie cry a little.

"It's so embarrassing that we aren't wearing jeans," Kelsey whispers, so now I'm kind of embarrassed too. Kelsey says she feels like everyone's staring at us, but I don't see anyone even looking at us. "Those girls over there," she whispers. "Don't look! They were *just* staring at us."

I miss our cafeteria. I miss Ms. Olsen, I miss Mr. Brazil. I even miss Ms. Brownstein. I miss our playground, I miss the dinosaur and the chestnut tree and the green slide. I miss the soap in our bathroom that smelled like SweeTarts.

In middle school, all the kids are giant and all the classrooms look the same, and there isn't one single soft chair anywhere in the whole building!

In middle school recess is called break, and we don't have a playground, we have a courtyard and a field. The courtyard has a basketball hoop and bike racks and a tetherball pole without the tetherball so it's just a pole. There's a wall covered in tiles with art and words on them, LOVE and PEACE and JOY, but mostly we just have concrete.

In middle school everyone cusses. Even the girls. Even the F-word. The girls don't play, they just walk around the

I wonder if middle school is when you stop playing.

Polly's pinching up sprinkles and sucking them off her fingers.

After the sprinkles are gone she'll lick off all the frosting, then she'll ask if anyone wants the rest of her donut.

"Can I *please* just go to my room?" Tana doesn't even want her donut. She *has* to have a donut. It's our tradition. We all have to eat donuts and talk about our first days.

"Just ten minutes," Mom says, and Tana says, "Fine" and drops down onto her chair.

I want to say *terrible* when Mom asks about my day but if I say *terrible* I'll have to say why and I don't really want to say why so I say, "Good," which isn't really a lie because the Jell-O was good. "Kelsey's in my homeroom. And the Jell-O's great."

"I knew you'd love it," Mom says. "Tana, if you aren't going to eat it, leave it alone."

Tana gives her donut one more big flick with her fingernail. It almost flipped all the way over.

Polly's all sad because she's the only one of us left at Riverside and because her teacher said *Polly Alder* when all Polly did was tell Sadie what page they were on. But she liked PE. They got to wheel around on the wheely things.

Tana gets to share a locker with Harper but she doesn't like her math teacher (he gave them homework on the first day) and she hates her nose. "It's getting worse! I look like a pig!"

Mom says that's just ridiculous. "Did someone at school say you look like a pig?"

"See! You know I look like a pig or you wouldn't have asked me that! It's totally noticeable!"

"It doesn't even turn up that much," I say, which I guess was the wrong thing to say because now Tana's yelling louder than ever. "That just proves it! It *does* turn up! I *do* look like a pig! I might as well move to a farm where I belong!"

We know we shouldn't laugh but that just makes it harder not to laugh, and then Tana smiles a little, which we thought meant it was okay to laugh but when we laugh

Tana says she hates us all and she never wants to see us again as long as she lives.

"Let her go," Mom says, even though we already know better than to follow Tana when she's mad. We listen to her stomp up the stairs and down the hall, we listen to her slam our bedroom door, then open it again so she can slam it even harder.

Mom says it's just hormones and it will happen to us too, which I already know from health class, I learned it last year, but Polly doesn't learn it for two more years so maybe Mom was saying it for Polly. Or maybe she doesn't know what I know.

"Polly, take your hair out of your mouth. You're using the shampoo, aren't you?"

"Yeah." Now Polly's painting her face with the wet hairs.

"I know you don't want me to cut your hair."

"Don't cut my hair! Please don't cut my hair!"

Polly says she promises she'll stop but I think it's like me with counting. It's not like you can help it, it's not like you even *want* to do it, it's like your body does it all on its own.

"Oh Polly," Mom says, "what are we going to do with you?"

I know she would say it to me too if she could see inside me.

"Anybody want the rest of my donut?" Polly's lips are all pink and there's a sprinkle stuck to her chin.

Mom says next time we go to the donut shop she's going to say, *Frosted donut, hold the donut*, but now she has to explain what *hold the* means!

Oh Polly.

Front door locked, kitchen door locked.

Kitchen window closed, basement door closed, living room windows closed, sliding glass door locked. Nobody behind the bathroom door, nobody hiding behind the shower curtain, bathroom window closed. Nobody behind our bedroom door. Nobody in the closet. Nobody under our bunks or under Tana's bed. Bedroom window closed.

Please don't let the murderer kill us, please don't let the murderer kill us. Please let middle school get better, please let middle school get better.

I'm holding the flashlight and Polly's holding me.

We were already in bed but Tana said *closet* so now we're having a closet meeting. The murderer's picture is in the newspaper that Tana snuck upstairs. We have to sneak read the paper because whenever Mom sees us looking at it she tells us to stop thinking about that man. She says there's no way he's coming back to our neighborhood so we might as well worry about a truck falling on our heads. Then I have to say, please don't let a truck fall on my head, please don't let a truck fall on my head.

I don't really like closet meetings because it's dark in here and it feels like all the clothes and shoes are trying to grab me, and if I accidentally touch a shoe I have to touch it again, and then I have to touch another shoe two times with my other hand, and sometimes it seems like the whole time we're in the closet I'm touching shoes!

"'An investigation,'" Tana whispers, "'is under way after a thirty-two-year-old woman was fatally shot at a North Eugene Mini Mart. Police say the suspect entered the market just before 4 PM Monday. The victim, Amy Gerding, was behind the counter when a man wearing a dark blue coat and a tan baseball cap entered the store.'"

I don't know what Tana said after that because I was thinking about Amy Gerding, because I just remembered something. After she said, *You girls having some lunch today?* she winked at us.

"'He allege-whatever asked for a pack of cigarettes,'" Tana says, "'and when Ms. Gerding opened the register he fired his weapon, killing Ms. Gerding instantly. A witness—'"

"What's *witness*?" Polly whispers.

"Shhh! 'A witness who saw—'"

"Just a person," I tell Polly.

"*Shhh!* 'A witness who saw a man running from the store just after hearing a gunshot described the suspect as medium build with dark brown hair pulled back in a ponytail.'"

I just remembered something else! Amy Gerding's earrings. They were flip-flops, little pink flip-flops.

"'The suspect fled the scene on foot, heading east on Elm Avenue. Police believe drugs may have played a role in the incident.'"

"What's *incident*?" Polly whispers.

"*Shhhh!*"

"I'll tell you later," I whisper.

Now Tana's reading all mad. "'A second witness who saw TV reporting of the incident said she saw a man fitting the suspect's description at a West Eleventh Wendy's restaurant.'"

"That would be weird if he was just sitting in there drinking a Frosty."

Tana keeps reading but she isn't telling us what it says.

"What? What's it say?"

"Oh my God," Tana says.

I try to see the words but Tana pulls the paper away.

"Tell us!"

"*Shhhh!*"

"You have to read it out loud!"

"You can read it after me."

"Come on, Polly, let's go to bed."

"Fine," Tana says. "It says the police think he's hiding with friends or family."

"Why would somebody be friends with a murderer?" I say.

Polly says, "The murderer has a mom?"

I can't even find Arkansas on that thing.

All the states are the same green color, green and brown. Ms. Olsen's map was a lot nicer.

Mr. Rickets is sitting on his desk like he always does, with his arms crossed. Hailey thinks he looks like Hugh Jackman but it's only because of his whiskers, and that's what Hailey says about any old person she thinks is cute.

So far six people have been to Disneyland, one person went to Disney World, two people went to Yellowstone park, and one person went all the way to France, but France doesn't count because it isn't in the United States.

It's Gordy's turn to stick a pin in the map but Gordy doesn't want to say the farthest place he's gone so now it's this kid Jayden's turn. When Mr. Rickets hands us a pin, we're supposed to say our names.

Jayden went to Memphis. He saw the actual balcony where Martin Luther King Jr. got shot. He was just standing on the balcony and someone shot him.

Some kids from Riverside look at Gordy when Jayden says *shot.* The kids from Emerson don't know about it, but all the kids from Riverside do. On September 23, Gordy Morgan turns twelve and his dad's giving him a gun. He already knows how to shoot it because last year he shot a deer. I heard him telling this boy Alex about it, how he shot her right in the neck. "How would I know that!" Tana said when Polly asked if she had babies. I never thought about her having babies. I hope she didn't have babies.

Everyone groans when Mr. Rickets asks if we all know about Martin Luther King Jr. "Okay, okay," he says, "just checking. But let's think about this. Imagine back before the Civil Rights movement, before desegregation." *Desegregation*, he writes on the board. "Well, for one thing, Alissa and Damon wouldn't be allowed to go to school here, right? They couldn't swim in the same swimming pool as us or go into the same restaurants. They couldn't even drink from the same water fountain."

I already heard all those sad things in grade school and I don't really want to hear them again, but at least I'm not

Alissa or Damon because everyone would be staring at me right now while Mr. Rickets tells us about Martin Luther King Jr.'s dreams and Rosa Parks refusing to move to the back of the bus.

I wonder where Martin Luther King Jr. got shot.

When I raise my hand Mr. Rickets points to me and says, "People, when I call on you, say your name. It's going to take me a while to learn all of you."

"Maggie."

"Maggie, what's your question?"

"Where did he get shot?"

"In Memphis," Mr. Rickets says. He says it like I haven't been paying attention, but that's not what I meant, I meant where in his body. Like in his head? Like in his heart?

Jayden's just standing there holding the pin he's supposed to stick in Memphis so Mr. Rickets says, "Memphis, anyone?"

Audrey's hand goes up. She says Elvis Presley's mansion's in Memphis. "I think he got shot too." All the Riverside kids look at Gordy again.

"Actually," Mr. Rickets says, "Mr. Presley died of a heart attack."

Audrey says he had a jungle room. "And he liked banana pudding. And burnt things."

"No way," this other girl says. I don't know her name

but I think she might be one of those girls who thinks she knows everything. "He didn't eat burnt things."

"He did! He ate burnt toast and burnt bacon."

"I heard he shot himself," Kirby says. "I think he shot himself in the head or something."

Mr. Rickets says he is nearly positive it was a heart attack. "But people, let's get back on track."

Gordy keeps his hand down low on his desk so I don't think Mr. Rickets even notices when he turns it into a gun and shoots the whiteboard. I don't know if you can get in trouble for that anyway. It's not like it's against the rules to pretend shoot something, and pretending doesn't mean you would shoot something for real.

"A baby!" Polly shouts the tiny way she shouts.

Mom says Polly's shouts are like bird chirps. I'm a goat and Tana's an elephant.

Polly's on her knees looking through the crack at the bottom of the fence because she likes to see all the rabbit poop under Mr. Gullick's cages. Tana was sitting on the back steps listening to her music but now she's looking through the crack. "Ew, it doesn't have any fur!"

We've never seen a baby before, not a baby little as that. The mother rabbits keep them hidden away, that's what Mr. Gullick told us one time. The mothers pull out their fur to make soft little nests for their babies.

We take turns seeing if we can reach the baby with our fingers but our arms aren't long enough so Tana gets a stick.

"Be careful!" I say.

"Don't poke her!" Polly says.

"I'm not poking her! I'm pushing her!"

"Don't push her too hard! Don't hurt her!"

"I'm not hurting her!"

When the baby's close enough, Tana doesn't want to touch her so I get her with my finger and pull her through the crack.

Her skin's all gray and pink. She looks more like a mouse than a bunny. Polly puts her hands under my hands and we carry her inside to show Mom.

"We found a baby!"

Mom's sitting on the couch studying. I hold the baby over her garden book so she has to look.

Polly's doing her jumping-up-and-down thing. "We found her! We found her!" and Tana has to move way over by the TV so she won't get whacked by flapping arms.

Mom's smiling, I think she likes the baby. I think she thinks she's cute. "Where in the world did you find her?"

"In the poop!" Polly says, jumping, flapping. "In the poop!"

We tell Mom about the crack at the bottom of the fence and about Polly seeing her and Tana getting her with a stick.

"Can we keep her?"

"Can we keep her?"

Tana says, "We could keep her in our room." (I didn't know Tana even liked her!)

"She can stay in our room!"

"She can stay in our room!"

Mom says she isn't ours to keep, she's Mr. Gullick's. "Besides, we don't know how to take care of a baby bunny, not a newborn like this. Polly, please stop jumping."

Polly stops jumping but then starts again when I say, "You can look it up on the computer!"

"You can look it up on the computer! You can look it up on the computer!" Now Polly's doing her crisscross feet.

"I'm pretty sure I know what the computer will say. Babies need to be with their mothers. It will also say that I have a test tomorrow that I'll fail if you girls keep interrupting me."

Mom's going to college on the computer. She's going to be a landscaper. First she's going to practice on our yard, put flowers all over the place. It's going to be like that part in *The Wizard of Oz* when Dorothy opens the door and everything's in color.

We don't want to give the baby back to Mr. Gullick but we don't want her to miss her mother so we sit on the back steps taking turns holding her, taking turns rocking her in our hands, singing *rockabye bunny in the treetop,* singing *hush little bunny, don't say a word,* until we hear Mr. Gullick's screen door creak open and bam shut.

It started raining a little so we make our hands into a house to keep the baby dry on her way back to her mom.

"That there's the runt," Mr. Gullick says. "Mother must've pushed her out of the nest."

"She needs to go back," I say. "She needs to be with her mom."

"Can't go back now. Mother won't take care of her."

"The dad can take care of her!" I say, but Mr. Gullick isn't listening, he's looking around the cage. He just said a bad word, he said *hell*. "How the hell?" he said. "Guess I must of grabbed her when I was cleaning out the cage." He hangs his arm over the fence and opens up his hand. "Let's have her back now."

"The dad can take care of her!" I say again.

"Ho no, the dad might eat her."

"Then we'll take care of her," Tana says.

"We'll take care of her!"

"We'll take care of her!"

I hold the baby against my neck where she can't get eaten up. I keep her there even when Mr. Gullick knocks his knuckles on our side of the fence and says, "Come on now, I have work to do."

I only turned my head for one second, I was looking at our house, I was thinking of running but my feet wouldn't move, then the baby was gone. It happened like a magic trick. One second she was behind my ear and the next second she was all closed up inside Mr. Gullick's fat pink fingers.

Now my feet are running, they're running so fast into the house, into the living room, into Mom on the couch, right on top of Mom's stupid garden book. I don't care if our yard ever looks like Munchkinland! "The mother won't feed her!"

"The daddy will eat her!" Polly says.

We tell Mom every word Mr. Gullick said. "'Ho no, the dad might eat her,'" Tana says in a mean man voice. "'Come on now, I have work to do.'"

Mom says it's very sad and she wishes she could do something. "I really do, but I can't tell Mr. Gullick how to raise his rabbits."

Tana elephant shouts, "So you're just going to let him kill her! That's what he's going to do, he's going to murder her!" She scrunches herself all up in Dad's chair, and Polly cries her *whys* into Mom's arms. My shouts and cries are all stuck inside me, so I'm just hugging Polly hugging Mom and watching Tana pray. I hope she prays a good one. I hope it works.

We sit there all sad and quiet until Mom says, "How about we have a little ice cream?"

We don't yell *ice cream!* like we usually do, we don't yell for syrup or sprinkles, we just follow Mom into the kitchen and wait for our bowls.

After our ice cream, when we're in our room, when we're all three piled on Tana's beanbag chair and Tana isn't pushing us away or yelling at us to get off, I tell them about feeling Mr. Gullick's fingers tickling my hand. How it was like my fingers opened up all on their own. I tried to keep hold of our baby, I wanted to keep hold of her, I just couldn't.

If the baby dies, it's all my fault.

All the doors and windows are locked.

Nobody's behind the shower curtain or in our closet or under our beds. I'm up in my bunk saying the things that will keep us all from dying and keep the baby bunnies safe when someone knocks on the front door. Before I even have a chance to worry about who it's going to be, Mom's opening up the door, saying, "Gordy? Come in, sweetie." She called Gordy *sweetie*! Now she's saying, "It's okay, the girls are in bed." The door just closed so I guess Gordy's in our house now. Gordy Morgan is *in our house.*

Tana was saying her prayers and Polly was blowing her nose but now we're all quiet. Tana says *shhh* and gets out of bed, so Polly and I get out of bed too. We slide our socks behind Tana's socks, across the floor, into the hall, over to the stairs. We sit down so slowly, it's like we're afraid our legs might creak. We lean our ears over our knees but we can't hear anything because Dad's in the bathroom and he just turned on his toothbrush.

Tana holds her finger to her lips and slips her bottom over the steps until she's halfway down the stairs. I go next, then Polly, then we're three heads hanging over our knees, trying to hear why Gordy Morgan's at our house.

"I don't want Gordy Morgan at our house," Polly whispers.

It sounds like Gordy's crying but we don't know why, then Polly coughs so now Mom knows about us sitting on the stairs. "Girls! Back to bed!"

We follow Tana up the stairs but we don't go back to our room. We lie down on our stomachs at the top of the stairs and listen for more.

We can hear talking but we can't hear words over all Dad's brushing and spitting. They're in the kitchen so probably Gordy's getting a snack because he's sad. Maybe cocoa and cookies.

"Do you think he killed someone with his gun?" Polly whispers.

"He doesn't have his gun yet," I whisper so quietly I can barely even hear myself. "His birthday isn't till September twenty-third, remember?"

We want to stay awake until Gordy leaves, we want to ask Mom why he's at our house, but Dad comes out of the bathroom and tells us to get to bed. "Shhhh!" we say, but it's too late, now Gordy knows about us listening, even though we couldn't hear a single word he said!

At breakfast we stand around Mom while she flips the bacon and toasts the toast and spreads the butter.

"What did he want?"

"Why was he crying?"

"Why did he come to our house?"

"What did you say to him?"

"Let's get our breakfast on the table first," Mom says. But we're more questions at the cereal cabinet and more questions at the fridge. We are questions getting spoons and questions pouring milk.

While we eat our bacon and Honey Smacks, Mom says, "Gordy has a harder life than you girls. Gordy's mom isn't well."

"What's wrong with her?"

"Does she have the throw-ups?" Polly asks.

"Probably cancer," Tana says.

"No," Mom says, "not that kind of sick. She just isn't able to take care of her boys the way moms are supposed to."

"Like baby bunny's mom?" Polly says.

"What about Gordy's dad?" Gordy's dad is eating him up, he's chewing on Gordy's head.

"Well, he isn't a whole lot better than Gordy's mom."

I've seen Gordy's mom plenty of times. When we're walking by Gordy's house on our way home from school she'll be sitting on her front porch in her pajamas, smoking a cigarette or drinking her coffee. I've heard her yelling too. Sometimes it's the dog she yells at and sometimes it's Gordy, and sometimes I can't tell if it's the dog or Gordy. I've only seen Gordy's dad maybe three times. He isn't much taller than Gordy's brother Nate, and he has the same kind of sticking-up hair as Gordy except it's darker. Gordy got brown from his mom and straight from his dad. I wonder if he got their kind of sick too. I wonder if that's why Gordy is the way he is. And Nate. I heard Nate's even scarier than Gordy, but he's only mean to boys. He's a year older than Tana so he likes girls too much to beat them up. That's what I heard.

Tana says, "But why would he come over *here*? We aren't even friends with him!"

Mom says she doesn't know. "Maybe he didn't have anywhere else to go."

"So?" Tana says when I say Gordy Morgan knows we heard him crying.

"So?" she says when I say I bet he's so mad at us.

"Of course not!" she says when Polly asks what I was thinking: "Is Gordy Morgan going to shoot us?"

If I asked it, Tana would say, *Oh great*, but Polly's still little so she can ask things.

Gordy Morgan's sitting on top of the tile wall when Tana and I get to school.

"Hey!" he says, and jumps down.

We can't run for the school because he's blocking our way, so I grab on to Tana. I never noticed this before but Gordy Morgan has a fat chin.

"Tell anyone and I'll kill you," he says. Then he runs off to the blue doors. He throws the doors open so hard, one of them almost hits this older girl in the head! I don't know who she is, I think maybe Alicia's big sister, I think she's an eighth grader.

"Watch it!" she yells. *Right at Gordy Morgan.*

"See, he's just a little kid bully," Tana says, but I bet Gordy comes back out and punches that girl. Some other kids from Riverside are watching too, waiting for Gordy to come out and punch Alicia's sister, but he doesn't come back out, so now we're all watching Alicia's sister. Just digging around inside her purse. Just getting out her lip gloss and smearing it on her lips. Just smacking her lips together. Now she's flipping her hair all around like she's in a shampoo commercial.

I don't tell anyone about Gordy coming over. I don't even say his name. It's like I'm afraid Gordy Morgan will hear me and climb through our window and shoot us in our hearts.

"Nothing," I say when Kelsey says, "What's wrong?"

"Really?" I say, and try to look all surprised when she says, "Your face looks funny."

Kelsey says her mom wouldn't let her wear eye shadow but she's going to go in the bathroom and put some on and I can come with her and put some on too, but I don't want to put on eye shadow!

There are two other girls in here. They're making their eyelids purple and Kelsey's making hers blue but I can tell from the way Kelsey keeps looking at them that she wishes she had purple too. "Here," she says, "put some on." She hands me the little case but I just hold it while she smears pink glitter gloss on her lips.

I don't like my hair. It's too short, it's too straight. I look like a boy! I wish I had blond hair like Kelsey instead of dirt-colored hair. I wish I didn't have a big ol' gap between my teeth. I would trade my gap for Tana's nose any day. I doubt Tana would want a big ol' gap between her teeth, though. She'd probably say she looks like a donkey and should live on a farm. Hailey used to say she wished she had a gap like mine, but that was a long time ago and I don't even know if she was telling the truth. Maybe she was just being nice.

Also, I'm too short. But at least I'm not as short as Mia Fawler. As long as you aren't the *est* of something, like the shortest or tallest or fattest, it's okay, nobody even looks at you.

"You can wash it off before your mom picks you up," Kelsey whispers so those other girls won't hear. Now those other girls are putting on lipstick and smacking their lips together. After they leave Kelsey says, "You should come to the mall with me this weekend," but I know she isn't talking about going to get candy or samples from Hickory Farms, or going to the pet store to see the cats and hamsters.

Kelsey is my friend because when we were little our moms were friends, but we didn't become best friends until second grade. Kelsey is prettier than me, which I don't mind, but actually I'm kind of starting to mind because now it seems like Kelsey's *acting* pretty. Before it was just how she looked, now it's like her personality.

We wait until Mom's in the bathroom to look at the newspaper.

The paper was on Dad's seat. Dad's still at work, Dad's always still at work. Mom didn't even put a plate on the table for him.

The picture is black and white but Tana says you can tell Amy Gerding's hair is blond.

"No, she has brown hair," I say. "I remember, it was brown."

Tana accidentally spits out some potpie when she says, "Look, see? If she had brown hair it would be dark gray. If she had black hair it would be black."

I know I'm right, though, I know it was brown.

Amy Gerding had three kids. She had a five-year-old boy, a six-year-old boy, and a nine-year-old girl. She had a sister and an ex-husband. The paper says the murderer probably just wanted money but he panicked and that's why he shot her. Also he might have been on drugs.

"*That's* brown," Tana says, tapping the murderer's hair. Polly looks like she's afraid he's going to bite Tana's finger off. I don't like looking at him either. It's the same picture they showed on TV with his fat chin and his hair in a ponytail, but he looks even meaner now.

If Gordy Morgan's picture was in the paper he'd have dark gray hair and dark gray eyes. His hair would be sticking up on top and sweaty by his forehead and ears from all his running around, and his shirt would be white because he likes the white football team.

The suspect is Gordy Morgan, an eleven-year-old boy from Lincoln Middle School. His mom is sick and his dad isn't much better. He has a brother named Nate who never goes outside and a dog that won't quit barking, and on September 23 his dad is giving him a gun and he already knows how to shoot it.

It's Saturday tomorrow and Dad's taking us to the beach to look for driftwood.

I think it was Mom's idea. I think she's trying to cheer us up because we're still so sad about the baby bunny.

Mom was going to come too but then she decided not to. Probably Mom and Dad got in a fight. Probably they did it when we were outside so Polly wouldn't worry about them getting a divorce. I worry too but nobody knows it because I keep it in my stomach with everything else.

I like Mom and Dad best when they're at the beach because Dad's happy and Mom's pretty as a piece of driftwood. Dad doesn't say it and Mom doesn't tell the story, she never tells the story in front of Dad, but I know we're all thinking about it. When we were little, Polly and Tana and I used to say to each other, *You're pretty as a piece of driftwood* and *Why thank you!* and *Oh marry me!* and we'd pretend kiss and roll all over the sand laughing until we couldn't breathe. Sometimes I still whisper it to Polly, *You're pretty as a piece of driftwood*, and she falls down laughing, even though it isn't that funny, not like it used to be.

When Dad's gone on his long walks looking for driftwood, we play the dot game. We lie down on our stomachs and watch him get smaller and smaller, then we try to guess which dot is Dad. We say, *That dot's too tall! That dot's too fat! That dot has a dog!* Mom tells us to go play but we can't, we have to keep watching so we can say we were right, we knew that dot was Dad. When Dad's gone too long I'm sure he's drowned in the ocean and I have to say the words that will undrown him. Please don't let Dad drown, please don't let Dad drown.

Sometimes Dad walks us around the tide pools—Not tide *poles*, Tana says because Polly's always saying it wrong. Dad holds Polly's hand so she won't slip on the slimy rocks and I pretend slip so he'll hold my hand too. The game is to find something in the water and say *Look, Dad! Look what I found!* so Dad will come over and say *Hey, a starfish! Hey, a sea anemone!* Sometimes when he's being funny he makes up the names. *Hey, a wallahooza!* Or, *I don't believe I've ever seen such a fine specimen of blechy.* Things like that.

Dad just came in to kiss us good night. "Other cheek," I say because he never remembers to kiss both.

“I’m waking you girls up early so get some sleep.”

There’s no way I’m going to be able to sleep. I’m too excited about the beach and too worried about Gordy and the bunnies. And now I’m worried that I won’t fall asleep until late and then I’ll oversleep and Dad will leave without me! Please don’t let Dad leave without me, please don’t let Dad leave without me. Please don’t let Gordy or the murderer kill us, please don’t let Gordy or the murderer kill us. Or anyone. Or anyone. Please don’t let the moms throw their babies out of the nest, please don’t let the moms throw their babies out of the nest. Please don’t let the dads eat them, please don’t let the dads eat them.

We're outside early because Tana couldn't sleep.

Then I couldn't sleep because Tana turned on her light to read, then Polly couldn't sleep because she heard me asking Tana to turn off her light. Outside our window it looked like summer, all bright blue and sunny, like the best kind of sun, the kind that makes your arm hairs stick up, but when we got outside it wasn't warm at all. It was the worst kind of arm-hair-sticking-up sun. Plus the grass is getting our shoes all wet. Plus I just remembered the murderer! Please don't let the murderer shoot us, please don't let the murderer shoot us.

Polly says she wants to go back inside. "Fine," Tana says, "but Maggie and I are staying out here," so now I have to stay out here, and if I stay Polly will stay too.

We don't have anything to do so we just walk around the yard like squirrels, like three squirrels looking for nuts. But if we're squirrels we'd be running, not walking, so I guess we're more like crows, three big crows looking for worms, or maybe we're rabbits.

The babies! If a baby fell out of the cage, she'd be all wet. She'd be so cold.

Polly follows me to the fence. I get down on my knees so I can look through the crack. Now my pants are all wet, now my knees are all cold. I don't see any babies, but I can only see under two cages, I can't see under those other ones.

"Is there a lot?" Polly whispers. She means rabbit poop. "Can I see?"

I know I could see the other cages from that branch up there but I've never climbed the apple tree before. I've climbed the tree in the front yard but this branch is much higher. When Tana used to climb it she'd put her shoe on this bump, then she'd grab hold of that little leafy branch sticking out of the trunk and pull herself up, then she'd swing her leg over the big branch and keep pulling herself up until she was sitting in the tree.

I climbed the apple tree! I'm sitting in the apple tree!

The ground is very far away. The ground is a lot farther away than I thought it would be. What if I fall? If I fall, I'll break my arm. Maybe I'll break my leg. Maybe both my legs. What if I break my *head*? I think you can even die falling out of a tree. Please don't let me die, please don't let me die. I squeeze my knees around the branch and hold on tight to the trunk so I won't fall.

"Fine," Tana says. I don't know why she's saying fine but now she's stomping off.

The cages are too close to the fence so I can only see part of them, and the part I can see is blocking my view of the grass so I can't even tell if any babies fell out. I know I could see better from the end of the branch but I can't let go of the trunk or I'll fall and die.

"Grapes!" Tana yells. She's over by the grapes that Sam says are theirs but Mom says are on our property too. Mom says we get to eat the grapes just like Mr. Gullick gets to eat any of the apples from our tree that hang in his yard.

Sam lives in that yellow house next door. She has two sisters and two brothers. The girls are *S*'s and the boys all start with *D*. Sam, Shauna, Serena, Darren, Dave. They wear keys around their necks so they can get into their house after school. Serena wears eye shadow and Darren smokes even though he's only two years older than Tana. I can see part of Sam's backyard from up here too. There's a bike back there and one of those giant green squirt guns, the kind Mom won't buy for us because they look like war guns.

I can't see that much of Gordy's backyard because there's another tall fence between Mr. Gullick's yard and

Gordy's yard. If I lived right next door to Gordy, I'd build a tall fence too, I'd build an even taller fence. All I can see is Gordy's back door and some of his grass and half of his doghouse. There's a lawn mower in his backyard, even though it looks like nobody ever mows that grass, and there are pots with grass growing out of them. There's a brown hose and a baseball bat and a lawn chair, the kind you lie down on, with a lumpy thing on top of it, a big brown lump.

"Maggie! Grapes!"

The lump just moved! The lump is a sleeping bag and now the sleeping bag is sitting up. Gordy Morgan! Please don't look at the apple tree, please don't look at the apple tree.

"They're ready to eat!"

Gordy's getting out of his sleeping bag. He slept in his jeans and a T-shirt. Please don't look at the apple tree, please don't look at the apple tree.

"Maggie!" This time it's just little Polly chirps, but she's chirping right by the fence, right by where Gordy Morgan's standing on the other side! "The grapes are ready!"

Please don't look at the apple tree, please don't look at the—

Gordy Morgan just looked at the apple tree! He looked *right* at me. I think he's mad because he just yanked his sleeping bag off the lawn chair and now he's stomping inside his house.

I grab hold of the leafy branch and swing my leg over like I've seen Tana do. I slide myself down a little but my shoe can't find the bump. I don't like going down, going down is a lot scarier than going up! I don't want to let go but then I hear Dad's car starting up and Tana and Polly are running for the driveway and what if they all leave without me!

I landed on my feet! My legs didn't break! But now my legs are all shaky and won't run as fast as I want them to.

When I get to the driveway, Dad's car is gone but Tana and Polly are still here.

Tana says Dad was surprised we were up so early. Polly says Dad said, *You girls be ready when I get back.*

I don't tell Tana and Polly about Gordy Morgan. I don't even tell them why I climbed the apple tree. I don't know why, I just don't.

When we go inside, Mom's awake. She's sitting on the couch doing her I Ching. She doesn't tell us what she asked but the answer is *Treading upon the tail of the tiger, it does not bite. There will be progress.*

"What's treading?" Polly says.

Mom says treading is when you walk on something.

"Who would ever walk on a tiger's tail!" I say. "That would be the dumbest thing ever."

"Oops!" Tana says, all duh, "I accidentally stepped on a tiger's tail."

We stretch out our seat belts as far as they'll go.

I'm hugging Dad's headrest and Tana's hugging the one that would be Mom's if Mom came with us. Polly has her elbows on the part between the seats that has all the gum and sun-glasses inside it. We have Dad for a whole day and we're going to play horseshoes in the sand because Dad brought the horseshoes bag.

"Tell the horseshoe joke!" Polly says.

"Well," Dad says. "The first thing you have to do—"

"Is find a horse!" I shout.

Tana's mad, she says I ruined the joke, but Dad says he couldn't have said it better himself. Dad's in a good mood. He has his coffee. He said *Beautiful day for driving* when we were getting into the car, and before that he kissed Mom good-bye and told her to study hard, so I think they made up. Now Mom's only staying home because she has a test on Monday, not because she hates Dad.

"Actually," Dad says, "we better find two horses."

"Why?" Tana says. She's all happy again.

"Well, two players, right? And you can't play horseshoes unless each player has four shoes."

"Oh," Tana says. It's not that funny. It's not really a joke, it's more like math.

"A horse in tennis shoes!" I say like we used to say when Polly was little and didn't get the joke and always said, *But horses don't wear shoes.*

"No, a horse in high heels!" Tana says, so now Dad's making the horse clicking sound.

He makes it sound light and ladylike, and we can almost see that horse in her high heels. Then the lady horse starts running, *click-click click-click*, just like when we used to sit on Dad's lap, when he'd say, *And this is the way the cowgirls ride.* We're laughing so hard we can hardly breathe, and I guess I was kind of bouncing up and down, like how Dad bounced me on his knee, and I guess I was shaking Dad's headrest, because Dad just said, "Maggie! That's enough." And we are back in our seats so fast, it's like we all three got shot.

For the rest of the trip we are quiet, we are three quiet girls reading our books so Dad will be happy again.

It's freezing out here!

We're wearing our winter coats, our hoods are up. Tana's lying on her back in the sand like she's in Hawaii. More like an Eskimo in Hawaii. Polly and I are lying on our stomachs, watching for Dad's dot, eating the Necco Wafers he gave us because he doesn't know we don't like Necco Wafers. I don't think anyone likes Necco Wafers. Necco Wafers are only good for playing Communion. We tried to get Tana to play but she said it's too cold to be a priest, so Polly and I are taking turns closing our eyes and sticking out our tongues.

"I see him!" Polly chirps, and Tana rolls her head to the side to look. "That's not him!" she elephant roars.

I almost yelled *Gordy Morgan!* because I thought that dot was Gordy, but there's no way Gordy's at the beach. I wonder if he ever goes to the beach or if he just has to lie on his bed in his backyard and pretend.

Now I'm kind of feeling bad for Gordy. I also kind of wonder if I would be mean like Gordy if I had a sick mom and dad who never took me to the beach. Maybe I wouldn't be mean like him but I'd probably be sad. Maybe sad turns into mean.

The dot turned out to be some old guy! I start laughing because it's so funny thinking about Gordy Morgan as an old man. "Nothing," I say when Polly asks what's funny. I wish I could tell Tana and Polly but it would take so long to explain all the crazy things in my brain. Like, isn't it weird that Gordy Morgan will be old someday? Gordy Morgan will be someone's grandpa. Grandpa Gordy.

"He's been gone forever," Polly says. "Maybe he fell in the water." So now I have to say the words *Please don't let Gordy Morgan drown—I mean Dad!* I can't believe I said *Gordy Morgan*! But now I have to say it again so Gordy won't drown either. Please don't let Gordy Morgan drown. Please don't let Dad drown, please don't let Dad drown. Or us, or us. Or anyone, or anyone.

I guess I was doing my staring thing because when I blink and can see again, Polly's staring at the side of my head and sucking on her hair. "You're pretty as a piece of driftwood," I whisper. Polly rolls over laughing, which makes me roll over laughing, but then all of a sudden Tana jumps up, which scares me half to death and makes me and Polly jump up too.

Tana chases us all around the sand, making kissing sounds and saying, "Oh marry me! Oh please marry me!" and Polly and I scream and run and leap over driftwood to get away, but I don't even want to get away because I love Tana so much right now! I love her so much I could marry her!

We're still running around when Dad comes back, so nobody won the dot game. Dad empties his bag of driftwood and we hold up the pieces and say what animals we think they'll be. Tana always takes the biggest pieces but I don't care, I like little animals and so does Polly. I make fish and Polly makes seal pups.

"Okay," Dad says after we've laid out all our animals and said their names a thousand times until their names became a song that Dad didn't want to hear anymore. "Which one of you horses brought an extra pair of shoes?"

It's Polly who jumps up first. She got the joke! She's even galloping over to the horseshoes bag. I wonder if quiet Polly will be funny one day. Maybe she'll even be loud. Maybe little seal pup Polly will turn into a sea lion. I wish I had a sea lion inside me but I think I might just be a fish.

Front door locked, kitchen door locked.

Kitchen window closed, basement door closed, living room windows closed, sliding glass door locked. Nobody behind the bathroom door, nobody hiding behind the shower curtain, bathroom window closed. Nobody behind our bedroom door. Nobody in the closet. Nobody under our bunks or under Tana's bed. Bedroom window closed. Please don't let Gordy or the murderer kill us or anyone, please don't let Gordy or the murderer kill us or anyone. Please don't let any moms push their babies out or dads eat them, please don't let any moms push their babies out or dads eat them.

Mom puts one of her old coats and two of Dad's old coats in a shopping bag for Tana to take to her friend Harper's church.

Tana says homeless people are God's people and Harper's church is going to give them coats so they can stay warm.

"Sort of like Uncle Rick," she says when Polly asks what God looks like. "Except not as fat. And his beard's longer."

Heaven is like a golf course except white. Like snow but warm. Kind of like whipped cream.

People are like balloons, helium balloons floating around. "Actually, more like astronauts," Tana says. "On the moon."

Polly and I moon hop around our room, but we don't float like we want to. "I can't wait for heaven," Polly says, so now I have to think it away. Please don't send us to heaven, please don't send us to heaven.

"Anything you want," Tana says when Polly asks what people eat there. "It's heaven."

"Candy?"

"Of course candy."

"Ice cream?"

"As many scoops as you want. And you never gain any weight."

"Mom's going to like it there," Polly says.

Tana is being all nice so we beg her to play with us. "*Please,*" I say. "*Please,*" Polly says.

Tana says she will but we have to hurry. Harper's picking her up for church any second now.

"Wonder Woman!" Polly says, and Tana says fine, but only if she gets to be Wonder Woman.

Polly's Wonder Dog and I say I'll be Wonder Girl but Tana says that's too many Wonders so now I'm Thunder Girl, which doesn't even make sense but it was the only thing I could think of with Tana looking out the window for Harper's car every two seconds. Plus I'm kind of scared of thunder, and how can your superpower be something you're scared of? There was this man, he was mowing his lawn and he got hit by lightning. It hit him right on the head and he died before he could even turn off his lawn mower.

Wonder Woman can freeze people and she has a net for catching them, and Wonder Dog has bionic teeth and superspeed. I pound on people with my feet and throw lightning at them. "They're the same thing!" I say when Tana says I'm thunder, not lightning. Dad told us. He told us thunder is the sound of lightning, it just comes later because light travels faster than sound. "Whatever," Tana says, which is what she says when she doesn't want to say I'm right.

I don't want to use my stuffed animals and Polly doesn't want to use her ponies so the bad guy is a pillow. Polly and I say the bad guy's Gordy Morgan but Tana says Gordy's just a stupid little boy and she can't believe we're still scared of him. I say I'm not scared even though I still am and I think Tana should be scared of him too (unless she isn't scared of *guns*) but I want Tana to play with us so when she says the pillow is the murderer I say okay.

I throw lightning at the murderer and jump up and down on him, but now Wonder Woman is mad because she can only use her net, because how can she freeze the murderer if he's just lying there on the ground. Wonder Dog says she wants to bite the murderer before Wonder Woman throws her net on him. "Fine," Wonder Woman says. "Bite."

Wonder Dog bites. She growls and shakes her head. Then Wonder Woman throws her net on top of the murderer and says, "Wonder Woman strikes again!"

"We need a name for all of us!" I say. "Like a team."

After Tana gets home from church we all go over to Grandma's house.

Not Dad, Dad had to go to work. Again.

Grandma is the oldest person I know. She could die any second. I can't look at Grandma without thinking about her dying any second. Especially when she's sleeping in her chair because when she's sleeping in her chair she looks dead. When she's sleeping in her bed she looks even deader because she takes off her wig and puts her teeth in a jar. Please don't let Grandma die, please don't let Grandma die.

Mom and Grandma are in the kitchen watching the news. We want to watch too because the newslady's talking about the murderer, but if we go in there, Grandma will make us tell her about school, so we're taking turns spying.

There's only one place you can sit where you can see the TV without Grandma seeing you.

While Polly's taking her turn spying, Tana takes out the heart. Operation is the only game Grandma has. She has puzzles but puzzles aren't really games, especially when they're flowers. I heard it buzz but Tana said it did not, so now she's trying for the funny bone.

Polly's back. She says she has no idea what that newslady's talking about but the murderer has a cute cat. "She's orange."

It's my turn. I crawl over to where I can see the TV on the kitchen counter.

The newslady says the murderer is Ray Scott. She's standing in front of a brown house. It's the house where Ray Scott's parents live. Ray Scott has parents. Ray Scott's parents have an upside-down boat in their driveway.

"When was the last time you saw your son?" the newslady asks.

"You get off my property," the murderer's mom says. "You get those cameras of yours and you get off my property."

Now there's a newsguy sitting on a couch. He says, "One special little girl and her efforts to save the manatees, right after this short break."

When I get back to Tana and Polly, Tana's waving the funny bone at me, and Polly's all hunched over, going for the charley horse but of course it buzzes right away. I tell them what I heard, about the murderer's mom telling the newslady to get off her property and about the girl who's trying to save the manatees.

"The manatees are dying?" Polly says, and I can already tell from her teepee eyebrows, she's going to want to save them. "Wait, what are manatees again?"

"Those things that look like hippos, they're like ocean hippos."

"They're super ugly," Tana says.

"No they aren't!" Polly says. "They're cute!" She runs into the kitchen even though it's Tana's turn, but Tana doesn't care because the murderer part is over. I'm trying for butterflies in the stomach even though it's practically impossible to get the butterflies out.

When Polly comes back, she's crying. "The manatees are dying."

Butterflies in the stomach buzzes so loud it buzzes my heart.

"So are the whales," Tana says.

"They are?"

"Tana, stop, you're making her suck her hair!"

"And the Bengal tiger," Tana says.

Polly already spent all of her money saving the seal pups so I don't know what she's going to do about those manatees. I don't think she has enough money to save even one manatee.

Mom's sitting on Polly's bed, talking to her about the manatees, telling her the manatees are going to be okay.

I feel bad that Polly's so sad, so when I'm all done saying the things that will keep us safe and keep the bunnies from getting pushed out of their nests, I add a prayer for Polly, even though it isn't really praying what I do. But for Polly I say, please don't let the manatees die, please don't let the manatees die.

The girl next to me, this girl Lexi, just threw a note on my desk.

I have no idea why she's giving me a note, she isn't even that nice to me. One time I saw her roll her eyes when I asked Ms. Morris a question. I think she might be wild. Her jeans are all cut up, like Gordy's dog got hold of them.

It isn't a note, it's a list. It says *Cynthia* at the top and so far six people wrote things. I know I'm supposed to write something next because number five is blank, but all of the things are so mean!

1. She wears the ugliest pants *ever.*
2. I think she makes them out of towels!
3. Does she ever brush her hair?
4. She totally needs braces.

I don't want to write anything but when I show the note to Kelsey, she says I better. I think Kelsey put on too much eye shadow today. I wonder if she knows, I wonder if I should tell her. She writes something on her notebook and pushes it to the edge of her desk so I can see. *Do you want them to do you next?*

One day after school I heard Cynthia telling Ms. Morris about her rabbit so I know she likes rabbits, but that isn't weird. I write it down anyway because Lexi will probably think it's weird. I write *5. She likes rabbits,* and pass the note to Kelsey. Kelsey laughs but I don't know if she's laughing because she thinks rabbits are a weird thing to like or because she thinks it's funny that I wrote *rabbits.*

Kelsey just showed me what she wrote. *6. She likes to eat them.*

Cynthia is opening her mouth, she's taking a bite out of the rabbit. The rabbit squeals so loud my eyes scrunch up. There's blood coming out of Cynthia's mouth.

Kelsey says, "Oh my God, you should see your face!"

Now everyone is looking at my face.

"Kelsey," Ms. Morris says, "is there something you'd like to share with the class?"

"No thank you."

"No thank you," Jake says in a super girly voice that doesn't sound at all like how Kelsey said it, and now a bunch of kids are laughing. I feel bad for Kelsey but I also know why it happened. It's because she was being mean to Cynthia.

Actually, I kind of think she was being mean to me too.

"Did you see Kelsey's eye shadow?"

"Yeah, I saw," Hailey says. We're waiting for Mr. Rickets to start class, we're watching him write *Life Skills* on the whiteboard.

"I think she's wearing mascara too."

Under *Life Skills* Mr. Rickets writes *Responsibility.*

"Do you think we should start wearing eye shadow?" Hailey whispers.

"*No,*" I whisper, a little too loudly so now a bunch of kids are looking at us. Practically everyone is looking at us.

Mr. Rickets stops his pen in the middle of *Respect.* "Ladies?" he says, and Hailey has to wait until he turns back around and starts writing *Resilience* before she can whisper, "Good."

Tana says she'll be Ray Scott.

"Maggie can be Amy Gerding, and Polly, you can be the news reporter. No, wait, you should be the news reporter, Maggie. Polly, you're Amy Gerding."

Polly has a whole ponytail in her mouth. She wanted to play Protectors and so did I but Tana said she'd only play with us if we played Murderer. "It's just a game," she said. "Don't be babies."

"Stand back there," Tana says, and Polly rocks like a penguin until she's behind the dresser that Tana pulled out from the wall to be the checkout counter. "Now act like you're selling Skittles or something."

Polly takes her ponytail out of her mouth and whispers, "Anybody want some Skittles?"

"Not like that! That's not how they do it in stores! You have to wait for me to come up and put my Skittles on the counter. See this comb? Polly, see this comb? You have to look! This comb's the Skittles, got it?"

Before Tana even puts the comb on the counter, Polly's wrapping her arms around her head and chirping the way she chirps instead of shouts, "Don't shoot me! Don't shoot me!"

"I'm just a customer! I just want to buy Skittles!"

"Don't worry," I whisper, "she won't shoot you. Just say, 'That'll be sixty cents, please.' "

"That'll be sixty cents—"

"*Bang!*" Tana yells. "*Bang bang bang!* Okay, now do the news report, Maggie."

"But she's crying! You scared her!"

"You can't cry, Polly, you're dead! Maggie, you have to do the news report.

"Fine," Tana says. "I'll do it. Today at four o'clock a man shot and killed a clerk at the Mini Mart. Witnesses say the murderer was buying Skittles when he pulled out a gun and shot the clerk in the heart."

I found a way to get to the end of the branch.

You just hold on to the high branch with one hand and scoot yourself out. But you have to hold on tight and go super slow.

I can see more of the grass in front of the cages but I still can't see all of it because the branch is too low and it doesn't go all the way to the fence. The high branch is the only branch that sticks into Mr. Gullick's yard. I know I could see everything from up there but I'm afraid it will break because when I pull down on it, it bends a little.

There's a pile of hay in Mr. Gullick's grass. I think he's cleaning out the cages.

"Are you cleaning out the cages?"

"Yup."

He keeps sighing. Grunting and sighing. It doesn't even seem like he likes his rabbits that much. "Do you even like your rabbits?" I didn't mean to say *even*! I meant to say it nicer.

Mr. Gullick stops all his shoveling or whatever he's doing over there. I thought he was going to get mad, but he just blows a bunch of air out his mouth and says, "Well, they're a lot of work."

I don't like the way he's throwing all that hay out of the cage. He isn't being very careful. He doesn't even like the rabbits so why would he care about throwing out a baby? "Are there any babies in that hay?"

"Babies are big enough now." He digs around in one of the cages and holds up a bunny for me to see. He doesn't hold her very gently. More like he's holding a rock or a bar of soap.

"Aw! She's so cute!" I say even though I can barely see her inside his big hairy hand.

Polly runs to the fence and Tana puts her magazine down and walks over, and we *aw* and *aw* until Mr. Gullick says he supposes we can hold her if we're real careful.

"We'll be careful," I say.

"We'll be careful," Polly says.

Tana gets her first because she's tallest and I still have to jump out of the tree. It's my best jump so far. I didn't feel it at all.

Aw. She's a little brown bunny with tiny, tiny ears.

Polly and I want our turns, we beg for our turns until Mr. Gullick says, "You all take turns now. Can't keep her over there too long."

"I wish we could keep her," Polly says.

"We should buy her!"

"Well, you'll have to talk to your mom about that," Mr. Gullick says. "Hold on now! Hand her over first."

Polly and I don't even wait for Tana to hand her back, we're already running for the house. "She's just going to say no!" Tana yells after us.

"I'll think about it," Mom says, same thing she says every time we ask for a cat. It's because Dad doesn't like animals (except driftwood ones), I know that's why, I know she won't really think about it, but we keep trying anyway. We promise and promise and promise to take good care of her.

"We'll feed her!"

"We'll clean her cage!"

"We'll do everything!"

When Mom says rabbits aren't cheap, Polly and I are so fast back outside, shouting all the way to the fence, "How much? How much, Mr. Gullick?"

Tana's sitting on the back steps reading her magazine. "I know she didn't say yes."

"She's going to think about it!"

Tana laughs her not very nice laugh. "Yep."

Mr. Gullick says thirty dollars. "I have thirty dollars!" I have thirty-five dollars. Polly gave all her money to the seal pups and manatees so she's going to pay me back after her birthday.

Polly runs inside to tell Mom, but I just thought of something. I can buy *all* the rabbits, then the babies will be right here in our backyard and I won't have to climb up to the high branch to protect them. I'll rake people's leaves to make money, I'll sell cookies. "How much for all of them, Mr. Gullick?"

I don't like the way Mr. Gullick laughed when he said, "*All* of them?" Like what I said was so dumb. "I don't think your mom would like that too much. Besides, Alderwood's ordered most of these here for the twenty-second. Except the younger ones. Not enough meat on 'em yet."

I don't hear what Mr. Gullick says next because my ears are pounding too loud, then my feet are pounding through the yard, then the door is pounding open and pounding closed, and it's like the whole universe is pounding when I yell, "Mr. Gullick kills his rabbits!"

“He kills them! Mr. Gullick kills the rabbits!”

I don’t wait for Mom to get off the couch, I don’t want her to hug me and say *Oh Maggie* and *Everything’s going to be okay* because it’s not going to be okay, how can it be okay?

Tana and Polly follow me up to our room and wrap all their arms around me until the pounding gets quiet enough for me to tell them what Mr. Gullick said. What he said about not even liking the rabbits. What he said about the babies not having enough *meat* on them yet. “We have to save them!”

Polly says we can buy them.

“We can’t! He already sold them to Alderwood’s!”

“What’s Alderwood’s?”

"That restaurant," Tana whispers, "that fancy restaurant where Aunt Sandra had her wedding party."

"I'm going to save them. I have to save them." I'm going to climb up to the highest branch and jump into Mr. Gullick's yard and save those rabbits.

Tana says stealing's a sin, but isn't she always telling us that God forgives sins? And isn't *killing* rabbits a bigger sin than *stealing* them? Tana says we can pray for God to take care of the rabbits in heaven. She puts her hands together and Polly puts her hands together. I put my hands together too but my prayer is different. God, please forgive me for stealing Mr. Gullick's rabbits. God, please forgive me for stealing Mr. Gullick's rabbits. Amen. Amen.

Something woke me up.

The rabbits! The rabbits need me!

It's very early, it's 5:08. Everyone's sleeping, everything's dark. I want to get back into bed but if I get back into bed something bad might happen to the rabbits.

The stairs creak a little but nobody wakes up. If Mom and Dad wake up they'll make me go back to bed. If Tana and Polly wake up they'll ask me what I'm doing. I don't like going downstairs without Tana and Polly but I have to. I have to make sure the rabbits are okay.

My shoes are so cold inside and my stomach doesn't want me to go outside. It isn't the same without Tana and Polly. The sky is all brown, the crows are all staring at me.

The murderer is long gone by now, the murderer is long

gone by now, the murderer is long gone by now, the murderer is long gone by now.

No babies under the cages.

The tree bump is slippery, my shoe almost slips off. I have to hurry before the murderer grabs my legs! My heart is so loud, it's thumping my whole body, it's thumping my ears and my neck and my stomach. I hold on to the high branch with one hand and scoot myself out. The farther I scoot the bendier the high branch gets. I'm glad I don't have to climb up there yet! It's only September 14 so I still have eight more days, and I already know what I'm going to do. I'm going to climb up to that branch and crawl out to the end, until I'm on Mr. Gullick's side of the fence, then I'll jump down—or maybe I'll climb down onto one of the cages and jump down from there. Now all I have to do is figure out what to do with all those rabbits. I can't just let them out. What if they get hit by a car? What if Gordy's dog eats them!

No babies in the grass.

Something just tapped me on the head! I almost screamed but then I realized it was only an apple. I've been so busy with the rabbits that I didn't even notice how big the apples are getting. They still aren't ripe—I had to turn and turn it about a hundred times to get it to snap off—and Mom says sour apples can give you a stomachache but I like them that way, I think they taste good. Plus they don't have wormholes yet.

I can see some of Gordy's sleeping bag. It isn't moving so I guess he's still asleep. I don't know why Gordy sleeps outside. Maybe it's because his parents don't take care of him the way parents are supposed to. I don't like Gordy but I feel bad that he has to sleep outside.

I was only thinking he might be hungry when he woke up, that's all. I was thinking he might want some breakfast, that's the only reason I threw the apple, I was thinking he would find it when he woke up. I didn't mean to *wake* him up.

Gordy just threw his book on the ground and now he's getting up! Now he's picking up the apple! Now he's throwing the apple at me! It almost hit me! I almost fell out of the tree! I want to climb down before he throws anything else but my legs and arms are too shaky, so I just keep holding on. Even after Gordy goes inside his house and slams the door, it's still forever before I can let go.

“*What are you saying* one two one two *for?*”

I didn’t know I was saying it out loud. I didn’t even know I was counting. I was too busy worrying about Gordy being mad at me.

At least it was Zach who heard me and not someone else. Zach isn’t mean and also he doesn’t care if you don’t answer his questions because he’s used to people not answering his questions.

“You sound like a soldier. Are you pretending to be a soldier or something?”

I kind of forgot about Zach. I’ve barely seen him around school. He must have stopped acting like a horse all the time like he did at Riverside because I would have noticed if he was galloping around the courtyard or going up to girls and making horse sounds. I hope people aren't mean to him here like they were mean to him at Riverside. "Are people mean to you here?" I didn't mean to say that! Why are my thoughts always leaking out?

"Not really," Zach says, which I think might mean yes. "Are they mean to you?"

I have no idea why he just asked me that. Kids aren't mean to me. Why would they be mean to me? Maybe they *are* mean to me and I just don't know it. "Are they?"

The other thing about Zach is, he stares.

"Yes," I say. I don't know why I said yes, I wasn't even asking myself. And I don't know why I was thinking about Kelsey when I said it, because Kelsey isn't mean to me, she's my friend!

Maybe now.

Gordy just threw the ball too far and Corey's running off to get it, so maybe now I'll go over there and tell Gordy that I wasn't trying to hit him, I only wanted to give him an apple. I'm going to do it, I'm going to go over there. But now Corey's back! Now I can't go over there.

"What are you watching those boys for? You have a crush on Gordy Morgan? Maggie has a crush on Gordy Morgan!"

Mom says you have to just ignore people like Sahara, but I don't want Gordy to think I have a crush on him so I turn my head a little like I was just watching those girls over there walking like they're in a three-legged race.

Gordy just said the F-word, he said F-off.

I thought he meant me but when I peek over there, he's looking at Sahara. It was Sahara he was telling to F-off.

When I go back inside, Kelsey's sitting in the hall talking to some girl with long black hair and ripped-up jeans. They're leaning against the lockers tapping their shoes together. I'm pretty sure that girl's a seventh grader, she might even be an eighth grader. I don't know how they got to be friends already but they're laughing like they've been friends forever. "Oh my God," Kelsey says, "that is *hilarious*." I have no idea what's so hilarious, but I think that girl's a popular girl because a bunch of other girls just ran over and now they're pulling her arms away with them. "Call me later!" she shouts back to Kelsey, and Kelsey shouts she will.

When they're gone, Kelsey says, "I *so* want a phone." She flips her hair back even though it isn't really long enough to flip, it only comes down to her shoulders. "Hi!" she says because two more girls just said hi to her. One of them is from Riverside so I don't know why she didn't say hi to me too. The other girl must be from Madison. I don't know how Kelsey knows all these people.

"Hi, Maggie!" It's Cynthia. I feel bad saying this but I wish it was someone else saying hi to me instead of Cynthia. Yesterday she wore Mickey Mouse ears all through math.

"Hi," I say, and I'm so glad she keeps walking. I think I might be blushing right now.

"Remember when we made those cell phones out of cardboard and candy buttons?" I don't know why I just said that. That was such a stupid thing to say.

"Oh yeah!" Kelsey says. "And we pretended to call each other. Until we couldn't stand it anymore and ate up all the buttons!" Now it's me and Kelsey laughing. Just like when we were kids.

I'm only on 28 seconds when Mom pulls into the parking lot.

There's a man with a ponytail and a fat chin walking into the grocery store but I can't tell Polly and Tana about him because I still have thirty seconds to go. If I hold my breath for sixty seconds Mr. Gullick won't kill the rabbits and nobody will get shot.

I hit Tana's arm and point at the murderer but Tana just says, "Ow! Stop hitting me!"

"Oh good," Mom says, "eggs are on sale." She cracks our windows and locks our doors and says she'll be back in a minute, even though she's never back in a minute.

As soon as she's gone, Tana unlocks her door. She pulls up hard on the lock so we all know how much she hates it when Mom treats her like a baby.

"The murderer," I say when I get to sixty seconds. "He went into the store."

"I seriously doubt it," Tana says, but then why is she chewing on her thumb?

Mom's in the store a long time. All she had to get was cake mix for Dad's cake.

"She's probably looking for candles," Tana says.

Polly takes her hair out of her mouth and says, "And eggs. Eggs are on sale."

I'm holding Polly's hand because she put it on my lap. "Look, see all those people coming out? That means Mom's okay."

"Why?"

"Wouldn't they be screaming if the murderer was shooting people?"

The man with the fat chin! He's coming out of the store! He's carrying a grocery bag. He's carrying a jug of milk. "There he is!"

"His chin's not fat," Tana says. "The murderer's chin is way fatter than that."

"I think it's fat," Polly whispers.

We're looking the other way when Mom opens the passenger door and drops the grocery bags on the seat, so I kind of scream a little.

"I hope you girls weren't fighting," Mom says while she's buckling herself in. "Here, keep these away from me."

A bag of corn chips comes flying over her seat and lands on my lap. "Thank you, Mom!"

"Thank you, Mom!"

"Thank you, Mom!"

I can't get it open, it isn't opening.

"That isn't how you do it," Tana says, "you have to *pull* it. Give it here—"

"I can do it," I say even though I can't. I have no idea how to open this thing.

"Maggie, give it to me."

Tana opened it up, all right. She practically ripped the bag in half, and now we're all covered in corn chips. We're eating corn chips off our laps, eating corn chips off our seats, banging our heads against the front seats to get corn chips off the floor.

Mom turns up the radio to listen to the news. There was an accident on the highway. A semitruck flipped over. There were casualties.

"Dead people," Tana whispers, but I already knew that. I was already thinking about the dead people, I could see all their dead feet sticking out from under the semitruck.

"Someone hand me up a few of those corn chips," Mom says.

"That's too many," she says when we all three pile chips into her hand, but she doesn't give any back and now she's driving one-handed, and what if a truck flips over, how's she going to turn the steering wheel with one hand? "Aren't they good, Mom?" I say so she'll eat faster, so a truck won't turn over and land on us. Please don't let a truck land on us, please don't let a truck land on us.

I got Dad a piece of wood to carve and Tana got him a Bible to save his soul.

Polly's crying because she doesn't have anything to give him. "Your love is more than enough," Mom says, but I think most people like presents on their birthday. I don't say it to Polly, though, because it will just make her cry harder.

We made Dad chocolate cake even though I'm sure he likes white cake better and Tana said he definitely likes banana cake best. "No, I'm pretty sure he likes chocolate," Mom said, but she didn't look pretty sure.

We shook blue sugar sprinkles onto the top but they just looked brown on the brown frosting.

"Wait!" I have an idea. I don't say the idea because I don't want Tana and Polly to steal it. I go to our room, I pull my box of animals out of the closet. Where's the seal, I can't find the seal. It has to be the seal because Dad likes sea animals. I found it! I run my seal down the stairs but I run too fast and trip. I'm falling down the stairs! My arms and legs are breaking, my head is cracking open. I am dead.

"Are you okay?" Tana says in her Mom voice.

"Are you okay?" Polly says in her My Little Pony voice.

"She's frozen again," Tana says in her Tana voice. "Oh my God, look at her eyes!"

I blink my eyes to unfreeze myself, I blink them again. My knees hurt and one of my elbows hurts but I'm not dead. "For the cake," I say, and hold up my seal. "For on top of Dad's cake."

Now Tana and Polly want to put things on Dad's cake too. Tana goes upstairs and comes down with a plastic flower that I know she pulled off one of the hair clips she used to wear. Polly has one of her ponies. I don't care, though, because Dad likes sea animals, not ponies and flowers.

We wait by the door while Mom gets the table ready because Dad's going to be home any minute.

"What if he doesn't come home?" Polly whispers.

"It's his birthday!" I say. "He has to come home!"

Tana says, "We should pick some flowers for him." But we don't have time, he's going to be home any minute.

Tana goes outside anyway, so Polly and I go outside too.

* * *

No babies under the cages.
No babies in the grass.
No Gordy in his backyard.

While we're looking for flowers, Sam comes over with a giant bag of chocolate chips. She's wearing the cutoff jean shorts she wears practically every day, even in the winter, except in the winter she wears them with these big furry boots. She shakes some chips into her hand and shoves them into her mouth. "What are you guys doing?" she says while she's chewing so we can see how chocolaty the inside of her mouth is.

Polly starts to tell Sam we're looking for flowers but before she gets *flowers* out of her mouth, Tana says, "Just hanging out." I know Tana doesn't want us to tell Sam about Protectors or Wonder Woman, but I don't know what's so wrong about looking for flowers.

I can't believe Sam gets to eat a whole bag of chocolate chips. "Your mom lets you eat the whole bag?"

"Duh, I stole it." She shakes a bunch of chips into her hand. "You can have five each."

They look like good chocolate chips. They don't have any white on them.

"Fine," Sam says. "If you're scared of some little chocolate chips."

"Why would we be scared of *chocolate chips?*" I say.

"We aren't scared!" Polly says.

Tana just rolls her eyes.

Sam opens her hand and we count out five each. I eat four and when Sam and Tana aren't looking, I give one to Polly so we'll both have even.

I don't think it's stealing because we didn't do the stealing, we just ate what got stolen, but when we're swallowing our chocolate chips Sam says, "Ha-ha, you ate them, now you're criminals!" and runs back over to her yard.

Sometimes I wish Sam wasn't our neighbor but at least she's better than Gordy. If Gordy lived next door I could never go outside because Gordy would be throwing things at me all the time or siccing his dog on me and I know I wouldn't be fast enough to get away.

Polly looks worried and Tana starts praying, but it's the shortest prayer ever, her eyes are already open again. She says she asked God to forgive us too, even though it isn't like we sinned. "Stealing candy's nothing. God forgives much bigger things than stealing chocolate chips, God forgives everything."

"What about the murderer?" Polly says. "Does God forgive murderers?"

"Of course not the murderer! He killed someone! He's going to burn forever in eternal flames."

I'm glad Polly asks about eternal flames because I was wondering too.

"It's like a big campfire," Tana says. "Like when we make s'mores except bigger, and except the marshmallows are people and they can't ever get out of the fire."

Tana picks three of Mom's orange lilies. "She won't care because they're for Dad." I pick some of the little blue flowers that grow in the grass.

"Those won't work," Tana says, "they're too little, they'll just fall inside the vase," but I don't care because they're my favorites and I'm pretty sure they're Dad's favorites too.

"Dad likes them."

"How do you know?" Tana says.

"He told me."

"No he didn't!"

I shouldn't have said he told me because everyone knows Dad doesn't talk about flowers.

We go inside to put our flowers in water. Mom puts Tana's lilies in a jam jar and my blue flowers in a bowl and Polly's little white flowers in the skinniest vase she can find but the stems are too short and floppy and the flowers keep falling out.

Tana says mine look like they're drowning to death but they do not, they're floating on top of the water. I think they look pretty and so does Mom. "Like a pretty blue carpet," Mom says. I tell Polly she can put her white flowers in my bowl so now it's a pretty blue-and-white carpet.

"How about you watch one show," Mom says. "I'm sure Dad will be home by the time it's over," but as soon as she says that, we hear Dad's key unlocking the door. Dad's home!

"Surprise!" Tana yells, and runs to the door. She didn't tell me and Polly we were going to yell surprise. "Surprise!" we yell. "Surprise!"

Mom was already at the door and I think I saw her kiss Dad on the lips.

We grab Dad's arms and jump up and down so it's like Dad's jumping up and down too.

"Hey," Dad says. I thought he was going to tell us to stop jumping around but he didn't, he said, "Thanks, girls."

We keep jumping, jumping and shouting, "Happy birthday! Happy birthday! We made you a cake! Happy birthday! A chocolate cake!"

"Okay," Dad says. "Okay now."

We pull his fingers to the table.

"We made it," Tana says.

"I put the seal on top!"

Dad says he loves seals.

"I put the flower!"

"I put the pony!"

"Very nice," Dad says.

I knew he would like the seal best.

Mom cuts big pieces and we all start eating, except for Tana, Tana is praying.

Dad says, "Why is Tana praying?"

"Why don't you ask your daughter," Mom says, but Dad doesn't ask, he just pokes up another bite of cake.

Dad likes his cake. We know he likes it because he said *mmmm* after his first bite and *delicious* when we asked if it was a good cake, and he ate his whole piece, he even smashed up all the little crumbs with his fork.

Front door locked, kitchen door locked.

Kitchen window closed, basement door closed, living room windows closed, sliding glass door locked. Nobody behind the bathroom door, nobody hiding behind the shower curtain, bathroom window closed. Nobody behind our bedroom door. Nobody in the closet. Nobody under our bunks or under Tana's bed. Bedroom window closed. Please don't let Mr. Gullick kill the rabbits, please don't let Mr. Gullick kill the rabbits. Please don't let Gordy or the murderer kill us or anyone, please don't let Gordy or the murderer kill us or anyone. 1, 2, 3, 4, 5, 6, 7, 8, 9, 10, 11, 12, 13, 14, 15, 16, 17, 18, 19, 20, 21, 22, 23, 24, 25, 26, 27, 28, 29, 30, 31, 32, 33, 34, 35, 36, 37, 38, 39, 40, 41, 42, 43, 44, 45, 46, 47, 4849505152535455565758596O.

"Stop panting!" Tana says.

"I'm not panting! I'm breathing."

"Stop breathing!"

Please don't let me stop breathing, please don't let me stop breathing.

I pick the black marker, the one that smells like licorice.

I put it by my bed so I won't forget.

I trained myself to wake up early. All I have to do is close my eyes and say, *Wake up at five o'clock, wake up at five o'clock* four times in a row and I wake up at five o'clock.

5:13. Well, thirteen minutes late isn't that bad. It's still early, everyone's still sleeping. Oh no! Thirteen! I close my eyes and count to sixty to make it fourteen because I do not need any bad luck right now.

Quietly so I won't wake up Polly and Tana, I climb down from my bed. I slip on my sweater and sneak on my shoes. I don't have any pockets for the marker so I stick it in my sock.

If you don't want the steps to creak, you have to skip the third step and the sixth step and the one at the bottom. If you don't want anyone to hear you open the door, you have to turn the doorknob as far as it will go and open the door fast before it can creak, then close it fast but not all the way, that part you have to do slowly so it doesn't make a *click*.

It's cold out here. It's colder than yesterday. My stomach doesn't want me to go outside, it never wants me to go outside.

Please don't let the murderer get me, please don't let the murderer get me. Please don't let the murderer get Mom or Tana or Polly either, or Dad at work, please don't let the murderer get Mom or Tana or Polly either, or Dad at work.

No babies under the cages, that's good.

The tree is very wet, it's very slippery. Please don't let me fall out of the tree, please don't let me fall out of the tree.

There are only three apples I can reach. I pick the best one. It doesn't have any bruises or holes. I can't let go of the high branch or I'll fall so I put the apple on my lap while I get my marker out of my sock, while I pull the cap off with my teeth. I squeeze the apple between my knees so it won't move when I write.

To, I write, but I think the marker's running out of ink, it's too light, I'm afraid Gordy won't see it. *TO*, I write bigger, *EAT*.

Gordy moved his lawn chair, it's against the fence now

so I can only see a little bit of him, maybe his head, maybe his feet.

I throw the apple but I don't think I threw it far enough. I think it's going to hit the fence.

It made it! It went over the fence. But now I'm worried it hit Gordy. I hope it didn't hit Gordy!

Gordy's dog is barking. I think I hear Gordy say "Shhhh," but I'm not sure because his dog and my heart are making too much noise.

On Friday we have to act out a play.

Social Studies is *not* my favorite class anymore. Mr. Rickets said we're going to divide up into four groups. I hope Hailey's in my group. I hope Gordy is *not* in my group. The parts are:

EROS: young god of love

PSYCHE: beautiful mortal princess

APHRODITE: goddess of love and beauty

KING: Psyche's father

SISTER: Psyche's conceited sister

ZEPHYR: the west wind

SERVANT

Please let me be the west wind, please let me be the west wind.

I'm nervous for Hailey too because she's so shy. She won't even raise her hand in class. And don't ask me why but I'm kind of nervous for Gordy Morgan.

Cynthia wants to know why I'm walking around the outside of the courtyard.

I can't tell her it's because I started walking around it and now I have to finish or there will be a hole in it so I say, "I just feel like it."

"But I mean why are you walking way around the outside like that?"

Hailey's sick and Kelsey's I don't know where and I didn't want to be the only girl sitting by myself and I didn't want anyone to see me walking by myself, but I don't want to tell Cynthia that either.

"Rabbit hair," she says when she sees me looking at her headband. "I gather it up after I groom my rabbit."

Now she's walking behind me, like we're walking on a

tightrope. And great, now I feel like I'm on a tightrope and if I don't walk super straight I'll fall off.

"How did you know I like rabbits?"

"What?"

"That note."

I almost fell off the tightrope! How did she know it was me? Did Kelsey tell her? I bet Kelsey told her. "What note?"

"I'm not mad, I just want to know if you like rabbits too."

If I say yes she might ask me to come over to her house and when you go to someone's house it's like you're all of a sudden friends, and if I'm friends with Cynthia I doubt Kelsey will still be my friend, Hailey but not Kelsey, because Kelsey thinks Cynthia is weird. I think she even said *totally* weird. Also, I kind of want her to go away right now.

"I have a Holland lop. She got second place at the fair. Second place in Youth Show, not Open Show, but next year I'm showing her in Open Show."

The bell rings and I still have to get back to where I started so I walk super fast, as fast as I can. I can hear Cynthia walking behind me, but when I finish and turn around to say good-bye, she's still walking around the circle, walking around it super fast, like maybe she has to get back to where she started too.

If that girl Lexi passed a note about me, it would probably go like this.

1. She has a giant gap between her teeth.
2. It's like the Grand Canyon.
3. She looks like a boy.
4. I heard she likes rabbits.
5. She's always walking around by herself.
6. That's because she doesn't have any friends.
7. Except for that totally weird girl Cynthia.
8. Maggie *is* a totally weird girl!

After school Polly wants to play Protectors of the Universe.

I kind of want to play too but Tana says she's busy. She doesn't look very busy, she's just lying on her bed staring at the ceiling.

"Shhh! I'm trying to think!" she says when Polly starts barking her Wonder Dog bark.

Now Polly and I are lying on Polly's bed staring up at the bottom of my bed.

"What are we thinking about?" Polly asks.

"Think what you want to think," Tana says.

Polly rolls her head my way. Her lips are orange, her breath is Cheetos. "What are you thinking about?"

"I can't think of anything."

"We don't know what to think about," I say. "What are you thinking about?"

"Fine," Tana says. "Boys."

When she's finally done thinking about boys she gets up off her bed and we follow her out of our room, but she goes inside the bathroom and locks the door. So now we're sitting on the floor waiting for her, waiting and waiting and waiting and waiting, but she never comes back out.

When Polly says, "I think she's combing her hair," Tana shouts a whole herd of elephants. *"Go away!"*

"Why's she mad at us?" Polly whispers.

"She's not mad, Pollywog," I say the way Dad says when he's trying to make Polly not sad about something, but I don't know how to explain what Tana is, and anyway I think Polly's too little to understand. They don't tell you about the mad-for-no-reason feeling until fifth grade.

I know what it feels like because sometimes I have it too. When people are being mean to each other, or when everyone's yelling and slamming their lockers, or throwing their lunch trays on the dirty stack, or for no reason at all, I feel like I could shout ten thousand goats.

But she doesn't always act that way.

Sometimes, in the dark, when we're in our beds, after she's done praying and before she falls asleep, I can whisper *Tana* and she won't yell *What!* She'll whisper *what* back, quiet like me, and I can ask her the things I want to know. About being older. About all the things she does now instead of the things she used to do. Like why she likes sitting on her bed more than playing in the yard and why she doesn't ever wear dresses anymore and why she paints her nails green and black instead of pink—and how could she just get rid of her entire horse collection? Mostly she says she doesn't know why, but one time she said it was just part of getting older. *It's not like you change,* she said, *inside. You're still the same person inside.*

In the dark I saw a littler Tana inside of bigger Tana, like the wooden doll at Grandma's house with the littler and littler dolls inside. I saw Tana who used to play Squirrel with us, Tana who played Pet Store and Dance Teacher and Lewis and Clark. I saw Tana the mama cat who purred in our baby kitten ears.

Sometimes I think about all the little me's inside of me. The me who used to put stickers on my face (even on my eyelids!), the me who kept a hurt slug in a box and cried so hard when he died. Me who was scared of Teletubbies. And sometimes I wonder when the me I am right now will get covered up by a bigger me, and I wonder who the bigger me will be.

All of a sudden Tana wants to go for a walk.

Mom's in the kitchen washing some pink meat in the sink. "A walk? It's a little late for a walk."

"*Please*," Tana says. "Just a little one?"

Polly barks her Wonder Dog bark—"*Ruff! Ruff ruff!*"—so Mom probably thinks we're playing a game, but I don't know if we're playing a game because Tana didn't tell us yet.

"We're eating in thirty minutes."

"Thanks, Mom!" Tana says.

"Thanks, Mom!" Polly and I say even though we don't know why we want to go for a walk.

"Where are you going!" Tana shouts when I run to the backyard. I just have to check on the rabbits, I have to make sure they're okay.

No rabbits under the cages.

"We're leaving without you!" Tana shouts before my leg is even over the branch.

"Wait!"

"Come on, Polly!" Tana says, but I know Polly won't leave without me. Tana would but not Polly.

No babies in the grass in front of the cages so I jump back down and run for the driveway, then Polly and I run to catch up with Tana. She's already past Sam's house, she's almost under the weeping willow. Maybe we're going to the duck pond. Except I don't think Tana likes looking for salamanders anymore.

Tana doesn't answer when I ask where we're going. She doesn't answer when Polly asks if we're going to catch salamanders, but the answer is no because we just turned the other way.

So far it isn't a very fun walk. We don't even have time to pick up acorns and I saw three good ones with their hats still on.

We're going too far. My stomach wants to go back. "Mom said not too far."

Polly was practicing her leaps but now she says she wants to go home.

Tana turns around so fast we almost run into her. "Gordy Morgan said you can see where Amy Gerding's guts hit the wall." Then she keeps walking so Polly and

I keep walking too, even though I don't want to see where Amy Gerding's guts hit the wall.

"I don't want to see Amy Gerding's guts," Polly says.

"Don't worry," I whisper, "it isn't true." Please don't let it be true, please don't let it be true. I bet it's just Gordy trying to scare us again.

"I think we should go back," I say.

But Tana just says, "If we walk fast, we can make it."

My stomach wants me to go back home. It's like there's a string coming out of my stomach and every time I take a step the string gets tighter. I'm afraid Tana will go a different way home and the string will get all twisted around trees and houses and I'll never be able to get it back inside me. "We have to go the same way home, okay? Okay, Tana?"

There are other kids at the Mini Mart too. Zoe and Karen and Karen's little sister, Maddy. They're looking through the window.

"Can you see it?" Tana says.

Zoe says she can't tell and Karen, who's always chewing on something, takes a plastic Smurf out of her mouth and says, "Let's go inside."

We walk like we walk through the haunted house, holding on to different parts of each other. Maddy's arms are wrapped around Karen's neck and Zoe's arms are wrapped around Maddy's neck. Karen's holding Tana's elbow and I'm holding Karen's elbow and Polly's hugging my arm, and all together like that we barely fit through the door.

It's the man with the accent working today. "Can I help you girls?" he says. I think he might be Indian or something, the India kind of Indian.

When we don't answer him he says, "There is nothing to see." I hear him say it again to himself when we're stuffing ourselves back out the door, except he says it sadder. "Nothing at all to see."

I'm the first one to spot Gordy Morgan and Corey Flynn. They're hiding behind a truck in the parking lot.

"You guys," I whisper, "don't look but Gordy and Corey are behind that truck. I just saw them, they were looking at us."

"I don't care if they're behind that truck!" Tana says, loud so Gordy and Corey can hear.

"Yeah, we don't care," Karen says, but we keep holding on to each other. We walk all stuck together out of the parking lot and across the street. We don't look back, even though we know Gordy and Corey are following us because they're laughing and saying things like, "Corey, I think those guts might have scared these little girls."

We try to walk faster but Maddy keeps almost falling down and I keep almost tripping over her. Karen is the first one to let go and start running, which is a big mistake, we were better together. As soon as she starts running we all start running and it's like Animal Planet when the lions get the slowest zebras. It's Polly and me and Maddy getting pelted with acorns and the green spiky balls that fall from the buckeye trees.

Polly's crying when we run through the kitchen door. "Gordy threw spiky balls at us!"

Mom hugs Polly and tucks her hair behind her ear so she won't start chewing on it.

"He's going to kill us!" Polly says.

"Spiky balls can't kill you," I say before Polly can tell Mom about Gordy's gun. If Mom finds out, she'll tell the principal and then Gordy will shoot us for sure. "It was just a game."

Mom says she didn't know games were supposed to make you cry, but I say it was fun. "Right, Polly?"

Polly nods, so I think it's okay, I don't think Polly will tell.

Do you think Gordy Morgan would really shoot us?

I don't ask Tana because Tana will just say, *Oh great.* I don't ask Mom because Mom will say, *Oh Maggie.* I don't ask Dad because Dad doesn't know Gordy, and anyway he isn't here. I ask myself, over and over, and wait for myself to answer.

"No," I whisper. "Of course not, stupid," I whisper. "Gordy Morgan would never shoot anyone." But I'm not really sure if I believe myself.

I thought Dad was at work but he was in Idaho.

His plane landed at 5:20 and it's almost nine o'clock. Mom says she should have gotten the flight number even though she already said that three times. She says she wishes Dad would turn his phone on even though she already said that about a hundred times.

We're sitting at the kitchen table eating Thin Mints. Mom likes Thin Mints because they're thin so they're better for you. She deals the Thins out like cards. One for Polly, one for Tana, one for me, one for her. Two for Polly, two for Tana, two for me, two for her. We have six Thins each. Polly and I nibble ours but Mom and Tana eat theirs whole. Tana closes her eyes first like they're giant Necco Wafers and we're playing Communion.

When Mom goes upstairs to get Polly a sweater because Polly's cold and too scared to go up there, Tana says, "What if his plane crashed?"

Polly looks at me and I shake my head no even though I was already thinking that. Last year an airplane crashed and everyone died. Even kids. Please don't let Dad's plane crash, please don't let Dad's plane crash.

"I saw you praying," Tana says.

"I wasn't praying."

"Then why were your lips moving?"

Mom's back with Polly's pony sweater. "You girls should be in bed," she says but she doesn't tell us to go upstairs so we stay at the table.

It's 9:23. The plane is falling into the ocean. There's a big splash and the plane goes under the water. The newsman says there are no survivors. Polly and Tana and I are standing in the cemetery where Grandpa's buried. We're wearing black dresses and shiny black shoes. We're holding black umbrellas. Tana's praying and Polly's hugging Mom's legs and everyone is crying.

It's 9:34. Nana's at the funeral too, but she isn't talking to us because Nana doesn't like Mom. Nana says Dad could have married the homecoming queen if he wanted to but he chose Mom instead. She never says it to Mom but she tells us, she tells us the homecoming queen liked Dad, everybody in town knew it. *Nice girl,* Nana says. *Skinny little thing too.*

"I hope he got us candy," Tana says.

Mom says she doesn't want us to be disappointed if Dad didn't get us anything. She says if Dad forgot she'll take us to the grocery store tomorrow and buy us some candy.

We already ate all our Thins and now we don't have anything to do so Mom gets out the pretzels.

The pretzel bag poked me on the wrist so now I have to poke my other wrist.

"Maggie," Mom says, "eat the ones in the bowl."

At ten o'clock we can't stop yawning so Mom says, "Up to bed." She doesn't come upstairs with us anymore, not until we're all ready for bed and it's time to kiss our cheeks.

I'm still saying the things I need to say to protect us and the rabbits, and Tana's still saying her prayers when the front door opens.

"Dad!" We kick off sheets, we jump out of bed. "Hi, Dad! Hi, Daddy! Hi, Dad!" We grab at each other's pajamas, we want to be first downstairs, we want to be first to hug Dad.

Dad's looking down at the floor and Mom's saying, "And you couldn't have called to let us know?" I wish she wouldn't have said that because now Dad looks all sad instead of happy to see us.

Polly gets to Dad first, she gets his stomach and both of

his arms, but then Dad pulls his arms out of her hug so now Tana and I each have an arm.

"Pretty late for three pretty girls to be up," Dad says. He's smiling at us but he still looks sad.

"We were waiting for you!" Tana says.

"We were waiting for you!"

"We were waiting for you!"

When Dad squats down, we squat too. When he opens up his briefcase it's like I'm opening up his briefcase because that's the arm I have hold of. Dad and I reach inside his briefcase and get out a crumply brown bag. We open up the bag. We reach inside and pull out three packages of rock candy.

"Rock candy!" I scream because I see them first, and now we're dancing, dancing the rock candy dance. Even Tana is dancing like she used to dance, and saying *Daddy* like she used to say *Daddy*, and laughing like she used to laugh when we were all little. We are all dancing and laughing and shouting, "Thank you, Daddy! Thank you, Daddy! Thank you, Daddy!" but Dad isn't even looking at us, he's looking at Mom, watching Mom walking away.

"Do you like my button?"

I take the longest time ever getting my books out of my locker because I don't really want to look at Cynthia's button right now. I know that's kind of mean but she keeps talking to me. *Every day.* I don't know why she isn't worried about getting to class. Class is going to start in two minutes!

"Don't you have to go to your locker?" I say, but she just pulls her shirt out so I can read the button. *Rabbit Feet Are Bad Luck.* I'm pretty sure she made it herself—actually, I'm definitely sure she made it herself.

"Do you like it?"

She did an okay job. Except maybe for her rabbit drawing. I think she wanted him to look like he didn't have any feet, but he just looks like he's taking a nap. "Um, yeah. It's cool."

"I'm trying to get people to stop buying rabbit feet."

"Why?"

"Because it's cruel!" Now she's following me down the hall, even though she doesn't have her books and her locker's the other way.

"But they aren't real. They're like bright orange. And purple." As soon as I say it, I feel so dumb. I just never thought about it before.

"That's what I used to think! But they *dye* them."

I'm also feeling kind of sick to my stomach because Cynthia is totally right, it's *so* cruel.

"Wait," she says, "you just gave me an idea! *Dye* and *die*. Get it? Like when people *dye* rabbit feet, rabbits *die*." Cynthia says she has a button maker and if I want to I can come over and make buttons with her.

I want people to stop buying rabbit feet but I don't really want to make buttons with Cynthia. "Yeah maybe," I say, and I am so glad the bell just rang before she could say when.

Kelsey said hi to me in the hall but now she's eating lunch with those other girls again.

Hailey says she doesn't care and I say I don't care either but I know we both care, I know we both wish Kelsey was sitting with us. We're not as fun without her. We're not as funny.

When we get up to empty our lunch trays Kelsey pretends like she doesn't see us, but I know she did, I saw her look at us and then look the other way.

Gordy just got up to empty his lunch tray too. He threw his lunch tray on the dirty stack without even cleaning it off first. Now he's watching me whacking my lunch tray on the side of the garbage can because I can't get these mashed potatoes to come off. His face is all red, red as Polly's handstand face.

"I'm not some poor starving kid," he says. "I'm not one of your stupid rabbits so you can stop trying to feed me." He turns away so fast he almost runs right into the lunch monitor, who I think was coming over to make sure everything was okay because she just gave me the *is everything okay* look.

"We were just talking." I can tell my face is handstand red now too.

"What was all that about?" Hailey whispers. "Why did Gordy say you were feeding him?"

"I'll tell you later," I whisper, even though I have no idea what I'm going to tell her. I hope she forgets to ask me.

Hailey doesn't want to go outside because it's raining, which I'm glad about because I need to do something. I just don't know what it is yet. "I'll meet you in the hall," I say. "By the library. I just have to do one thing."

"Tell you later," I whisper when she asks what I have to do.

Most of the girls are inside walking around the halls or sitting in the gym. I don't know where Kelsey is but I bet she's in the bathroom putting something on her face. I think she wears makeup-makeup now because her face is a different color, it's darker. It's kind of orange.

I just thought of what I can tell Hailey. I'll say I was throwing some food over the fence for Mr. Gullick's rabbits and I accidentally threw some in Gordy's yard. I'll tell her I had to go outside to tell Gordy it was an accident.

Mostly it's boys out here and the two girls who play basketball with the boys. Everyone's shooting baskets except for Gordy. Corey must be sick today because Gordy's throwing the football to himself. He throws it into the air like he's throwing it to a cloud or like he's throwing it to God. I never thought about it before, but I think Corey might be the only boy who hangs out with Gordy. The other boys used to but they don't anymore.

"I don't feed the rabbits," I say while Gordy's looking up, waiting for God to throw the ball back. My heart's beating so hard it feels like my stomach is beating too. "I save them. Mr. Gullick kills them and I'm going to save them."

Tomorrow we have to act out our play.

In six days Mr. Gullick is going to kill the rabbits. In seven days Gordy gets his gun. Please let me be the west wind, please let me be the west wind. Please don't let Gordy or the murderer kill us, please don't let Gordy or the murderer kill us. Please don't let Mr. Gullick kill the rabbits, please don't let Mr. Gullick kill the rabbits. 1, 2, 3, 4, 5, 6, 7, 8, 9, 10, 11, 12, 13, 14, 15, 16, 17, 18, 19, 20, 21, 22, 23, 24, 25, 26, 27, 28, 29, 30, 31, 32, 33, 34, 35, 36, 37, 38, 39, 40, 41, 42, 43, 44, 45, 46, 47, 48, 49, 50, 51525354555657585960.

"Do you have to breathe so loud!" Tana says.

I just saw Gordy Morgan go into the library.

Now he's talking to the librarian. I want to know what he's saying but I don't want him to see me so I stay in the hall, across the hall by the lockers.

I don't know what he just said but the librarian is smiling and I guess she said for him to follow her because Gordy's following her into a row of books, into *my* row of books, the row by the windows, the rabbit row, but I know Gordy isn't getting a book about rabbits, he's probably getting a book about guns, except why would the librarian be smiling if somebody asked her for a book about guns? Maybe he said war. But I don't think she'd smile for war either, so maybe he said hunting.

I was going to go into the library to see what book

Gordy got, I was going to act like I was looking for a book, but Kelsey just showed up and she wants to know what I'm staring at.

"I forgot," I say because I'm always saying stupid things like that around Kelsey.

"You forgot what you're staring at?"

It would be so weird if Gordy did read books about rabbits! I accidentally laughed out loud so now Kelsey wants to know what's so funny. There's no way I could ever explain what's funny about Gordy reading rabbit books, so it's a good thing one of her new friends came over and started talking to her. For once I'm actually kind of glad Kelsey has new friends!

I wish I had Hailey in my group. I wish I didn't have Gordy in my group.

I'm not that happy about Cynthia being in my group either because she looks way too excited about the play and she's wearing her rabbit-fur headband again and she keeps talking to me and that's probably why Claire was whispering to Audrey, they were probably whispering about having to be in the same group as the two weird girls.

Mr. Rickets said some girls will play guys and some guys will play girls, that's just how it's going to be. He barely even looked up from his paper when he gave us our parts. He just read out the parts and pointed at our heads.

I didn't get west wind, and I don't know if Mr. Rickets did this on purpose but most of the girls in my group got boy parts and most of the boys are girls. I'm Psyche's father and Gordy's Psyche's conceited sister and Cynthia's the servant. At least my part is small and nobody's really acting, we're all just reading our parts, even though Mr. Rickets said, "Come on, guys, this is a *play*, not an instruction manual."

We all have our scripts on our desks except for Gordy. Gordy's leaning way back in his chair with his pages on his stomach. He looks like he's about to fall asleep. After the narrator, he has to read his part. Audrey's the narrator. She just said, " 'Psyche's two older sisters sat nearby, weaving,' " so now it's Gordy's turn.

Gordy's looking at his paper but he isn't saying anything. "Go Gordy," Cynthia says. I can't believe she just said, *Go Gordy*! She tried to point to where his part was but he pulled his paper away.

Maybe he isn't a very good reader. Maybe he can't read out loud.

We're waiting so long for Gordy that a few people actually jump a little when all of a sudden he says in this super snotty girl voice, " 'So, Psyche, another day of marriage proposals? You must be exhausted.' "

At first nobody laughs, we aren't sure if it's okay. It kind of looks like Gordy's trying not to smile but it's hard to tell. It's Corey's laugh and Gordy's smile that get us all

Maya doesn't have any friends except for Polly.

That's why Tana and I got invited to her birthday too. Tana said, "But it's Saturday!" so Mom promised to take her to the mall after the party.

Polly talks about Maya the same way she talks about the manatees. She doesn't say Maya's cute but she's always saying *poor Maya*.

Maybe Polly's sad for me too because I only have two friends. More like one and a half friends because Kelsey hardly ever talks to me anymore.

Maya has a lot of drums in her living room and plants all over her house, even in the bathroom. I think they might be hippies. When we get home I'll ask Mom if they're hippies.

The birthday cake is on the kitchen table. The frosting

is gray and it isn't very smooth and there are pretzel sticks on top spelling *Happy Birthday*. Mom says, "I love it," even though there isn't much to love about that cake. Maya's mom says they have to be creative because Maya can't eat sugar.

I try to be extra nice to Maya because she doesn't have friends and she can't eat sugar. I tell her I like her dress even though I don't like it, except for the color, so it's not really a lie. "Purple's one of my favorite colors," I say.

"It's not *purple*," Maya says, "it's *plum*."

Maya says we're going to play now, so we follow her outside. Only part of Maya's backyard is mowed, the rest is a field. I don't like that it's crooked. I wish they mowed it even instead of crooked.

We're sneaking through the field part because Maya said she sees wild rabbits in here all the time and if we want to see them we have to be super quiet.

"See," Maya whispers, "that's why my mom put that chicken wire around her garden. Rabbits eat lettuce and carrots. Rabbits have good eyesight because they eat so many carrots." Maya is always telling us things we already know. I think that's one of the reasons she doesn't have friends. Plus her teeth. "There!" she whispers.

"Where?"

"*There!*"

"*Where?*"

"I don't see any rabbits," Tana says.

"*There!* Right *there*!"

The grass is moving but it could be a cat, it could be a snake. All I said was "What if it's a snake?" but I guess they didn't hear the *what if* part because now they're all screaming and running for Maya's crooked yard.

"Rabbit!" I see one. She's hiding in that clump of grass. But oh no, I scared her away. Where'd you go, little rabbit? I know you're in here somewhere. There you are! Aw, she's looking right at me. "Shhh, don't be scared, I won't hurt you." I think she likes me. She doesn't even hop away when I squat down. But now everyone's back, talking and staring and scaring my rabbit away.

"I bet the rabbits like it here," I say to Maya's mom when we're inside eating cake. It tastes more like a muffin than cake, more like bread.

Maya's mom smiles but before she can say how much the rabbits love it here, Polly chirps, "Piñata!" Out the window, in the backyard, Maya's dad is standing on a ladder, hanging a piñata in a tree.

Maya runs outside so we all run outside.

I think Maya's mom made the piñata too. It's yellow with orange triangles all around it. I think it might be the sun.

When Maya's dad reaches his arms up to tie the string around the branch, we can see some of his stomach under his shirt. I look away, into the field, so I don't have to look at Maya's dad's stomach. Some of the grass is moving. I bet it's my rabbit. I wish Mr. Gullick's rabbits lived in that field. Then he couldn't kill them. Then they'd all be safe and free.

"Maggie!" Tana's pulling on me, pulling me back. "Mom, Maggie's frozen again!" She says something about the piñata and I see the broom in Maya's hand, blurry because my eyes are stuck open. Maya's dad is saying, "The other end, the stick end," and everyone is laughing, but I don't care about the piñata, I don't care about the candy, I just want everyone to be quiet so I can figure out how I'm going to get Mr. Gullick's rabbits over to Maya's house.

There's a *crack* and everyone's diving for the ground. Maya made a hole on the first try, or maybe it wasn't the first try. Maybe it wasn't Maya. Tana and Polly are crawling around the grass, looking for the candy, and I hear Mom say, "What a great idea!" before Tana can say anything bad about the boxes of raisins and bags of peanuts and suckers that can't be real suckers because Maya doesn't eat sugar, remember?

Maya's parents aren't hippies, they just like drums and plants.

Front door locked, kitchen door locked.

Kitchen window closed, basement door closed, living room windows closed, sliding glass door locked. Nobody behind the bathroom door, nobody hiding behind the shower curtain, bathroom window closed. Nobody behind our bedroom door. Nobody in the closet. Nobody under our bunks or under Tana's bed. Bedroom window closed. Please don't let anyone kill anyone or anything, please don't let anyone kill anyone or anything. 1, 2, 3, 4, 5, 6, 7, 8, 9, 10, 11, 12, 13, 14, 15, 16, 17, 18, 19, 20, 21, 22, 23, 24, 25, 26, 27, 28, 29, 30, 31, 32, 33, 34, 35, 36, 37, 38, 39, 40, 41, 42, 43, 44, 45, 46, 47, 48, 49, 50, 51, 52, 5354555657585960.

This time when Gordy wakes up he doesn't go inside his house.

He stays in his yard and plays fetch with his dog. His dog is good at fetching but he isn't good at letting go. Gordy has to stick his fingers inside his mouth and shake the ball back and forth to get it out. Sometimes when Gordy throws the ball it hits Mr. Gullick's fence and scares the rabbits. I know it scares them because I can hear them going all crazy in their cages. I want to tell them, *Don't worry, little rabbits, in three days I'm going to get you out of those mean old cages and then Gordy won't scare you anymore.*

I wonder if Gordy has birthday parties. It's hard to imagine a bunch of people singing Happy Birthday to Gordy. I wonder if his mom gets him a cake. I can't imagine Gordy blowing out candles either.

"If you're so worried about those rabbits, why don't you do something about it instead of just staring at them all the time!"

I thought Gordy was talking to his dog because he was looking at his dog when he said it, but then he says, "Oh wait, I forgot. You're too scared."

Mom says she might.

I follow her upstairs to her bedroom. When she opens her closet I turn the other way because we're not allowed to look inside Mom's closet, it's where she hides our presents. Tana said she looked in there one time and it looked like the Bi-Mart.

"How's this?"

There's a shoe box on my shoulder. "Um. Well, I kind of meant a big box."

Mom takes the box off my shoulder and I can hear her moving things around, and paper crinkling like maybe some of the presents are already wrapped.

"I'm making something," I say, even though she didn't ask. It's not a lie because I am making something. It's for the rabbits. I'm going to put the box up against the fence to catch the rabbits when they hop through the crack. First I'm going to jump down from the tree into Mr. Gullick's yard. After I save the rabbits, after I get them out of their cages and they hop through the crack, I'm going to get on top of Mr. Gullick's cages and climb over the fence and jump back into our yard. I'll put the box of rabbits in the car. I'll hide it under a blanket. Mom won't even notice because the trunk is always full of stuff. I'll say I left something at Maya's house. My bracelet, my favorite bracelet. *I must have dropped it somewhere in the field*, I'll say when everyone asks where. While they're all looking around the field, while Mom's in Maya's kitchen talking to Maya's mom about all the plants in Maya's kitchen, I'll crawl out of the grass and sneak the rabbits out of the trunk and into the field. Then, when all the rabbits are free, I'll take my bracelet out of my pocket and say, *I found it!*

"Sorry," Mom says, "nothing big. Why don't you go look in the garage." She says I can use anything I find in there. I beg her to go with me but she says she's too tired. "Ask your sisters."

"A house for my stuffed animals," I tell Polly when she asks why I need a box. So now Polly needs a box too.

The garage is cold and dark and makes me have to go to the bathroom. Especially when I start thinking about the murderer running into the garage!

I sprint to the pile of boxes and grab the longest one I can find, the one that will make the best rabbit tunnel.

"That's a tall house!" Polly says.

"It goes the other way, the long way," I say, and run for the door.

"Wait!" Polly chirps. "Wait for me!"

Now we have two long houses.

In our room we gather all our stuffed animals. "I think they like it," we say. "I think they're cozy in there."

"But they can't breathe!" Polly says. "They need windows!"

I'm glad Polly said that because the rabbits will need to breathe too.

Our scissors aren't very sharp. We have to stab the cardboard to make holes before we can cut out windows. Polly makes big windows so her stuffed animals can see out. I feel bad that my stuffed animals don't have big windows, but I have to make my windows small so the rabbits can't get out.

"My windows are too big," Polly says.

"My windows are too small."

"My windows are stupid!" Polly says.

"*My* windows are stupid!"

Tana says it's hard to tell whose windows are stupider, so now we both feel bad about our windows.

"If he loves us so much, why doesn't he eat dinner with us anymore?"

I wish Tana wouldn't say things like that, and I wish she'd stop whacking her mashed potatoes with her spoon. They're already smashed into a pancake.

"First of all," Mom says, "Dad does eat with us sometimes—"

"Yeah right! Like when?"

"Second of all, Dad has to work so we can live in this nice house and eat mashed potatoes."

Tana's supposed to smile when Mom says *mashed potatoes*, and say *oh* like we always say *oh* about Dad not being home, but she doesn't, she says, "He hates us!"

Of course Dad doesn't hate us! Why would Tana even say that! Polly and I look at Mom, we're waiting for Mom to say, *Of course Dad doesn't hate us*, but Mom's just looking at Tana looking at her smashed-up mashed potatoes.

I take a bite of chicken. I take another bite but I can't get anyone else to quit their fighting and eat their chicken.

"I got an A on my spelling test," I say. I didn't even have a spelling test! It's just the first thing I could think of, but no one says *that's great*, no one even smiles.

"Tana," Mom says, "you know Dad loves you."

"If he loved us so much, he'd be here. He hates us! He hates *you*!"

Mom says we can talk about this after dinner.

"You're just saying that because you know it's true!" Tana yells. Then she's gone, running upstairs, slamming our bedroom door, then opening it again so she can slam it even harder.

"You know Dad loves you very much," Mom says, and Polly and I say we do, we know.

"And you too, right?" Polly says.

"Of course," Mom says. She smiles but it's more like a sad smile, more like an upside-down frown.

Please don't let Mom and Dad get divorced, please don't let Mom and Dad get divorced. 1, 2, 3, 4, 5, 6, 7, 8, 9, 10, 11, 12, 13, 14, 15, 16, 17, 18, 19, 20, 21, 22, 23, 24, 25, 26, 27, 28, 29, 30, 31, 32, 33, 34, 35, 36, 37, 38, 39, 40, 41, 42, 43, 44, 45, 46, 47, 48, 49, 50, 51, 52, 53, 54555657585960.

The thing is,

Tana keeps saying Dad's gone all the time but it kind of seems like she's gone all the time too. Not at dinner, but after dinner and after school and on the weekends when we're having our breakfast. She's always in our room, which doesn't even seem like *our* room anymore because if Polly and I make any sound at all, she tells us to go somewhere else. Maybe Tana's the one who hates us all. I really hope not, though, because then it would just be me, Mom, and Polly left. Or maybe just me and Polly, because sometimes when Mom's studying it kind of seems like she's gone too.

Rabbits are born with their eyes closed.

And their teeth never stop growing. The mother is called a doe and the baby is called a kit. The mothers pull their fur out to make nests for their babies, but I already knew that. Babies are born without fur. I already knew that too. Wild rabbits live in underground holes called burrows, and that's all I know so far because Ms. Morris just came over here and said break time is for socializing, not sitting in a corner reading books. Ms. Morris says she's noticed I haven't been spending time with my friends, but how can I spend time with my friends when I have to figure out how to save the rabbits? I only have two days to save them!

"You should get a Holland lop," Cynthia says. I don't know how she knew I was reading about rabbits. I put my knees up so she couldn't see the cover. "You can come over and see mine if you want."

"Thanks, but I don't think I want a Holland lop."

"What kind do you want?"

"I don't know. I don't even know if I want a rabbit."

"You can still come over. I'll let you hold Rainy."

That is the weirdest rabbit name ever. "Yeah, maybe."

"Really?" Cynthia has this giant smile on her face, and I didn't even say yes. All I said was maybe, and it was more like the probably-not kind of maybe.

"Why'd you name him Rainy?" I only asked it so she'd stop all her smiling at me.

Cynthia says it's because she looks like rain.

How can a rabbit look like rain?

"Well, more like a cloud that's about to rain."

"Wait, what's a Holland lop look like again?" I've never even heard of a Holland lop.

I thought Cynthia was going to say, *You don't know what a Holland lop is?* but she just said, "They have super thick hair and their ears go down instead of up."

So I guess she's a dark gray rabbit with ears hanging down.

So I guess maybe *Rainy* isn't so weird.

Cynthia just sat down at our lunch table.

I think she thinks we're friends now. Maybe I shouldn't have said maybe.

When she says hi, Hailey says hi back, and when Cynthia asks if Hailey likes getting hot lunches, Hailey says, *Not really.* Cynthia says, *The pizza's okay, though,* and Hailey says, *Except the sauce, it tastes like ketchup,* and when Cynthia says she doesn't mind because she loves ketchup, Hailey says she likes ketchup too but not on pizza. Like Cynthia sitting at our table is totally normal. Like we're all three all of a sudden friends.

I'm sure Kelsey is looking at us right now. Yep, I knew it.

"Why aren't you friends with that girl anymore?"

Great, Cynthia just looked at Kelsey so now Kelsey

knows we're talking about her. And why would Cynthia even ask me that? Of course I'm still friends with Kelsey! "What girl?"

"That girl you were just looking at! That girl Kelsey."

"We're still friends with her, we've been friends since we were little kids."

"Actually," Hailey says, "we aren't really friends anymore. I mean, right, Maggie?"

"I don't think she's very nice," Cynthia says. "Well, maybe she's nice, but she cares too much about being popular and that can make people not very nice in my opinion. It's just temporary, though. You can still be friends with her, after she grows up a little."

She sounds like a mom! And that doesn't even make sense! Kelsey's the one who's so grown-up. Kelsey's the one who puts makeup all over her face now.

"Eye shadow doesn't make you older," Cynthia says. (I am seriously worried that Cynthia can read minds.) "It just makes your eyelids look weird."

I see Hailey smile a little, which makes me smile a little. Actually, it makes me laugh a little, which makes Hailey laugh too, which makes Cynthia laugh three, which makes us all laugh even harder, and I don't even know why we're laughing, we should be sad about Kelsey.

For the rest of lunch, Cynthia asks us about two thousand questions, like what's your favorite condiment and if you could only eat one kind of sandwich for the rest of your life, what would you choose, and what do you think the lunch ladies cook at home, and do you think Ms. Arrington has a crush on Mr. Rickets, and even though she might be a little weird, and maybe even totally crazy, it's kind of like we're fun again, like how we used to be with Kelsey—before Kelsey started acting so young!

Gordy's talking about his deer again.

The one he shot. It's after school so everyone's in the hall. He's probably talking about it because it's almost his birthday, but he isn't going to shoot anyone because I'm going to save the rabbits.

At first I didn't see Gordy's brother, Nate. I don't think Gordy saw him either until Nate said, "You didn't kill that deer, Dad did." Nate's wearing a shirt without sleeves. He isn't much taller than Gordy but he's a lot musclier. Nate tells everybody that Gordy didn't cut that deer open like he said he did, and Gordy punches Nate in the chest for saying he just stood there blubbering like a baby until their dad made him go sit in the truck. Now Nate and Gordy are swinging for each other's faces and I think Gordy just got punched in the eye so I'm really glad that teacher came out in the hall to pull them apart.

Nobody says anything to Gordy but I hear some kids whispering about it outside, saying Gordy thinks he's so tough but he's just a crying little baby, he's just a bad-word, bad-word, bad-word.

Mom told us one time that when people
act big it's because they feel small.
I think that might be how it is with
Gordy.

I'm also thinking that if Gordy couldn't even shoot a deer, how could he ever shoot a whole person?

All of a sudden Tana doesn't like closet meetings.

I never liked going in that closet anyway so it's fine with me. Plus Tana's letting us sit on her bed. She's even letting Polly hug her pillow. On the front of the newspaper Tana opened up between our knees it says *Mini Mart Suspect Found.*

The murderer was hiding at the beach, he was hiding at his cousin's house. Now his cousin's in trouble too because it's against the law to hide a murderer in your garage.

"I don't think that's him," I say when Tana pushes the paper closer so we can see the picture.

Tana says he cut his hair so the police wouldn't recognize him but that's him for sure. "Look at his chin."

"He's even scarier without a ponytail," Polly says.

Tana's nails weren't all the way dry so now there's green

nail polish on the paper. She licks her finger and rubs at the green but that just makes it worse. Now there's a green cloud where the murderer's fat chin used to be. Without his chin and ponytail he kind of looks like Uncle Patrick but I don't say anything because I don't feel like hearing Tana say, *He does not*.

Wait. That means we were at the beach at the same time as the murderer! "Maybe he was one of the dots! On the beach!" I'm covered in a million goose bumps because I think I might have seen him. He was wearing a tan baseball hat. He walked right by us when we were watching for Dad.

Tana says there's no way he was one of the dots, but how would she know, she wasn't even looking.

"I saw him! He walked right by us!"

"No way," Tana says. "Why would a murderer just hang out on the beach where the police could see him?"

"I don't know, why don't you ask him?"

"Oooh," Tana says. "Look who's getting an attitude!"

I don't know what's so funny about it and I wish Tana would stop smiling at me because I don't want to smile, I want to be mad.

"First he followed us to the Mini Mart," Tana whispers in her super creepy voice.

Polly's already crawling on my lap, saying, "Stop! Stop it, Tana!"

"Then he followed us to the beach—"

"You're scaring Polly!"

"Then he followed us all the way home," Tana whispers, and puts her arms up so we know we're going to get grabbed as soon as she says the next part. Polly's like a koala bear wrapped around me.

"And now," Tana whispers.

"He's," she whispers, and wiggles her fingers.

"Following you up your armpits!" she yells, and Polly and I are screaming the screams that make Mom think our arms got cut off because the murderer is totally tickling us to death!

Mr. Gullick's killing the rabbits in two days! Gordy gets his gun in three days!

Please don't let anyone kill anyone or anything, please don't let anyone kill anyone or anything. 1, 2, 3, 4, 5, 6, 7, 8, 9, 10, 11, 12, 13, 14, 15, 16, 17, 18, 19, 20, 21, 22, 23, 24, 25, 26, 27, 28, 29, 30, 31, 32, 33, 34, 35, 36, 37, 38, 39, 40, 41, 42, 43, 44, 45, 46, 47, 48, 49, 50, 51, 52, 53, 54, 55, 5657585960. I'm getting better at holding my breath. I'm not even breathing hard.

There's a lady on the other side of the chain-link fence.

She's over by where moms park to pick up their kids. She's standing next to the dirty white car that's always parked in front of Gordy's house. "Gordon!" she yells. "Gordon Vance, you get your be-hind over here!" She's wearing a flowery nightgown and purple sweatpants underneath.

It's like freeze tag, like everyone in the courtyard got tagged. Hailey and I are frozen, everyone is frozen, staring at Gordy's mom. Except for Gordy and Corey. Gordy keeps throwing the football and Corey keeps missing it.

Mrs. B. walks over to the fence. I can't hear what she's saying to Gordy's mom but Gordy's mom's yelling, "Don't you make me come get you!" in this really scary voice. She sounds like a man. She sounds like a murderer!

Gordy keeps throwing the football like he doesn't even hear her, even when she yells, "I am not leaving here until that boy gets his lazy be-hind inside this car!"

Mrs. B. just called for me. I think because I was just talking to her, I was telling her that one of the tiles on the art wall is broken, LOVE has a crack in it.

I don't want to go over there, I don't want to get yelled at by Gordy's mom, but I have to. "Come on," I say, and pull Hailey with me.

"Girls, would you please go get Ms. Ranker?" Mrs. B. says in this really sweet voice, like it's not a big deal at all that Gordy's mom just yelled, "You better come find that damn dog of yours before I get hold of him!"

We run for the doors, we run down the hall even though there's no running in the halls. I don't know if Gordy will be mad at me for getting the principal, or glad. I hope he isn't mad.

When we come back outside with Ms. Ranker, Gordy's yelling at everyone to stop staring at that crazy bad-word, and he doesn't even know who that crazy bad-word is.

Ms. Ranker says something to Mrs. B. that makes Mrs. B. blow her whistle and hold up her arm. We all follow her arm to the green doors like a bunch of little grade-school kids, while Gordy's mom screams at Ms. Ranker for stealing her boy, and I don't know what everyone else is thinking right now but I'm thinking about the flames. I'm thinking about God. Wondering if he forgives people like Gordy's mom, or if Gordy's mom will be a marshmallow in the fire.

After school all the girls are whispering their oh my Gods *about Gordy's mom.*

I don't know where Gordy is but I hope he's somewhere where he can't hear them.

"He lives right behind Maggie's house," Kelsey says so now all the girls are looking at me, waiting for me to say something about Gordy's mom. Kelsey's popular friends too. Cynthia too. It's like I'm stuck inside a girl cave and I can't get out! I wish Hailey was here but I don't see her anywhere.

"He isn't right behind me," I say, trying to see over their shoulders, trying to spot Hailey. "The rabbits are."

"That's their *name*? *The Rabbits?*" At first I thought Keisha was asking if the rabbits were named *the rabbits*, but then I figured out she meant like a family, like the Rabbits family.

Kelsey laughs so some other girls laugh too, but I don't get what's so funny. I'm the only one not laughing. And Cynthia. Cynthia's just staring.

For a while everybody's talking and laughing about rabbits, but then this girl Ally says, "Is she always yelling like that?"

I can hear Gordy's mom yelling for Gordy to get his bad-word inside and Gordy's mom yelling for him to get that dog of his to shut-the-something up, so I don't know why I just said, "Who?"

"His mom!" about four girls shout at the same time, and they all laugh some more and one of the girls says, "Jinx!"

Something really terrible just happened to Gordy and everyone's just laughing and having a good time. I know nobody likes him, but still. "That wasn't his mom."

One of the girls, I don't even know her name, laughs like I'm just joking around but everyone else looks confused. Except for Kelsey. Kelsey looks mad. And except for Cynthia, who's just standing there looking at me with this big smile, which gets even bigger when I say, "I have no idea who that lady was."

I turn on the faucet so everyone will think I'm just brushing my teeth.

If I stand on the toilet and look out the window I can see Mr. Gullick's backyard but I can't see the cages because the fence is in the way. I can see Gordy's backyard but I can't see his bed, not even a little bit of his sleeping bag.

Mr. Gullick's killing the rabbits *tomorrow*, and Gordy gets his gun in *two days*! I feel like the world is about to end and I'm the only one who knows it. I'm the only one who can save us.

Gordy just came outside! He's walking around his yard. Now he's picking something out of the grass and throwing it to his dog. I think it's a ball. It is a ball because it just bounced and his dog caught it in his mouth. Now Gordy's grabbing his dog's head and giving him a kiss! Now he's throwing the ball again. Now he's yelling something at his house because the back door just opened. I can't see who it is but it's probably his mom.

Gordy just kissed his dog's head again and now he's throwing the ball really hard against Mr. Gullick's fence.

Now he's going inside his house.

Now he's gone.

"What are you doing in there?"

"Brushing my teeth!"

Tana doesn't even knock, she just walks right in. "That's how you brush your teeth? Standing on the toilet?"

"I'm looking at this spider. There's a spider on the window."

There really is a spider. There's a web too, up in the corner, a web with a poor little bug all tangled up.

"Are you feeling okay?" Mom says.

I guess I was kind of staring at my mac and cheese. Tomorrow morning, before anyone wakes up, I have to climb up to the high branch. I have to jump into Mr. Gullick's yard. I have to get all the rabbits out of their cages and through the crack and into the box. I have to climb on top of the cages and over the fence and back into my yard. I have to hide the rabbits in the trunk of Mom's car and hope Mom doesn't see them when she takes me to Maya's house, and hope they are quiet all the way there. I have to pretend like I'm looking for my bracelet in Maya's field, then I have to sneak back to the car to get the box and put the rabbits in the field when nobody is looking!

"Actually, I'm feeling a little sick."

Front door locked, kitchen door locked.

Kitchen window closed, basement door closed, living room windows closed, sliding glass door locked. Nobody behind the bathroom door, nobody hiding behind the shower curtain, bathroom window closed. Nobody behind our bedroom door. Nobody in the closet. Nobody under our bunks or under Tana's bed. Bedroom window closed. There are so many things I'm worried about I could never even say them all. Please let everything be okay, please let everything be okay. 1, 2, 3, 4, 5, 6, 7, 8, 9, 10, 11, 12, 13, 14, 15, 16, 17, 18, 19, 20, 21, 22, 23, 24, 25, 26, 27, 28, 29, 30, 31, 32, 33, 34, 35, 36, 37, 38, 39, 40, 41, 42, 43, 44, 45, 46, 47, 48, 49, 50, 51, 52, 53, 54, 55, 56, 57, 58, 59, 60.

After everyone's asleep I sneak back downstairs.

I put my rabbit box behind the couch so I won't have to carry it downstairs in the morning. I put my stuffed hippo inside the box so if Mom sees it she'll just think I was playing, even though I don't play with my stuffed hippo anymore but she probably doesn't know that. In the morning I'll put some carrots and lettuce in there. I already hid a little pile in the fridge behind the milk.

Mom said she'd take me to Maya's house tomorrow to look for my bracelet. "If they're home," she said. She tried calling Maya's mom but no one answered. Please let them be home, please let them be home.

"Maggie?"

Mom!

She's coming down the stairs!

"Maggie, are you down there?"

"I just had to check something!" I have to get to the stairs before she gets to the bottom and sees the box. What if she opens the refrigerator and gets out the milk and sees my pile of carrots and lettuce? "Hi, Mom!"

"Wow," Mom says when I put my arm around her and walk her back upstairs with me, "aren't you getting tall."

It rained last night, my shoes are soaked, the tree is wet and cold.

I forgot to look at the clock but I think it's very early because it's really dark out here and my stomach wants me to go back to bed right this minute. I don't think my stomach is going to like it when I climb up to that high branch.

Tana never climbed any higher up so I don't know how to do it. The high branch bends a little when I pull on it but I keep pulling until I can get my feet up on the low branch, I keep pulling until I'm squatting like a frog in the tree. Please don't let me fall, please don't let me fall. Then I straighten my legs a little bit and a little bit more until I'm standing.

I can almost see all of the grass in front of the rabbit cages. I'm so high up I think I'm going to be sick. My legs shake when I swing one of them over the high branch. My arms shake when I hop off the low branch and pull myself up. Please don't let me fall, please don't let me fall.

I'm up on the high branch! I can see everything! I can see the cages! I can see all of them! But it doesn't feel right, it's way too bendy, it doesn't feel right at all. Please don't let me fall, please don't let me fall.

All I have to do is get to the end of the branch and jump down into Mr. Gullick's yard, but the more I scoot the more the branch bends. Please don't let me fall, please don't let me fall. Please don't let me fall, please don't let me fall. I say it two more times and two more times and two more times and two more times. And then I fall.

First my arms break.

Then my legs.
Then everything is quiet.
My head is broken.
I am dead.

It was the crack that woke up Gordy.

That's what he told us when Mom brought him to the hospital to see me.

"The branch, not her leg!" he said when Polly made a face.

Polly was sitting on Dad's lap and Tana was leaning on Dad's back. Mom was sitting on my bed playing with my hair, tucking my hair behind my ear, but I didn't say, *Do the other ear.* I don't know why, I just didn't. Gordy was leaning against the wall. We tried to give him a chair but he wouldn't take it.

Mom said Gordy opened the door and yelled inside the house for them.

Gordy said he climbed over the Gullicks' fence. He held

up his arms so we could see all the scratches. I have no idea how he got over those fences! They're way too high to climb.

Mom said, "Dad had already left for work," and Dad said, "I should have been home."

"First I made sure she wasn't dead," Gordy said.

Mom said I was out cold.

"But you were breathing," Gordy said, "so I knew you weren't dead."

Dad said he should have answered his phone. He said he came as soon as he heard the message but he should have answered his phone.

"It's a good thing your friend here knew to keep you still," the nurse said. She called Gordy my friend! "You never know when there's a spinal injury."

Gordy said he learned about it from *Chicago Fire*.

"I was going to carry you to the car," Mom said, "but Gordy said no, so I called 9-1-1."

Everyone laughed when Polly said, *"9-1-2, that won't do."*

The fence is what broke my leg. First I fell on the fence, then I fell on the rabbit cages, then I fell into Mr. Gullick's yard. That's what they think happened anyway.

Mom and Polly and Tana followed the ambulance to the hospital. Dad came after my cast was on, when I was eating my Popsicle. He said, *My poor Magpie.*

When they went home to get my pajamas and toothbrush, Gordy was sitting on our front porch, so Mom asked him if he wanted to see me. Mom said Gordy said yes, but Gordy said he didn't say yes, he said, *I guess so.* He turned handstand red when Mom told everyone he was worried about me.

Everybody kept thanking Gordy, even the doctor, even Dad, and Gordy kept saying it was no big deal, it was nothing, but I knew it wasn't true, I knew it was something. I think it's like what Mom's always saying about how people act big when they feel small, except the other way around. All I know is, I never saw Gordy act so small.

I don't really care that Kelsey didn't call.

I wasn't really expecting her to. And I sort of figured Cynthia would call. And she did. Hailey told her what happened and now she's going to make me something for my cast (probably something out of rabbit fur!). Hailey came over as soon as I got home from the hospital. She brought me a milkshake. She also brought me homework. Which I kind of knew she would.

We make our legs into fences.

Three legs and one cast, even though we don't really need fences because our rabbits are just sitting there eating their carrots.

We're covering up my cast with grass. Gordy tried to put an apple on there but it just rolled off. "To eat," he said, and handed it to me. He was smiling when he said it, but still, I think I turned the same color as that apple.

On the way home from the hospital, Gordy and Polly and me in Mom's car (Tana went with Dad), Gordy told us how I let a bunch of Mr. Gullick's rabbits out. When I said *I did not*, Gordy said *You did too.* I said, *I was trying to but I fell.*

Yeah well, you landed on a cage. He said it was more like one long cage because they were all nailed together or something, so when one fell, they all fell. *Rabbits all over the place.*

I was worried I hurt them but Gordy said, *Nah. They were hopping okay.*

We didn't find out until the next day, when Mr. Gullick came over with our rabbits, that there was one cage that didn't fall. It was the only one that wasn't stuck to the others.

I told Mr. Gullick that I was sorry about all his cages, which wasn't really a lie because I said *cages* not *rabbits,* but he said it was okay, he was just about done with rabbits anyway. *Too much work.* He was going to give the last of them to his grandkids, but he saved one for me and one for Gordy. He even gave us the cage that didn't break.

Gordy's going to keep his rabbit with mine so his dog doesn't give her a heart attack. "Or my mom," he said. He laughed a little when he said it but it was kind of a sad laugh.

Dad's going to make some kind of rabbit thing for us out of driftwood, maybe a rabbit cave, he stayed home today so he can work on it, and Mom told Mr. Gullick she would plant some flowers where his cages used to be. She said you can't buy better fertilizer than rabbit poop. When she asked him what his favorite flower was, he said camellias, which I thought was so funny. I don't know why, I just never thought about someone like Mr. Gullick having a favorite flower. But I never thought about someone like Gordy liking rabbits either.

I already named my rabbit but so far Gordy's only come up with really bad names. He keeps naming his rabbit other animals. Dog, Cat, Turkey, Hippo.

"Tiger," he says.

"You can't name her Tiger! She's too sweet to be a Tiger."

"Okay, that settles it. Come here, Tiger! Come here, girl."

Gordy's mom is yelling for him to come home and now his dog's barking too. Wait, I just remembered it was Gordy's birthday yesterday! I can't believe I forgot. I almost said *Happy birthday* but then I remembered that the only reason kids know about Gordy's birthday is because of his gun and I don't want him to think I'm like all those other kids. I wonder if he got a gun. I wonder if he got a cake. I really hope he got a cake.

"You think all those other rabbits will be okay on their own? The ones that got away?"

Gordy looks like he's trying to pull up our whole yard. I think it's because his mom just yelled at him to get his bad-word over here before she whoops his bad-word. " 'Course they will," he says.

"How do you know?"

There's a hole in the yard where Gordy pulled out a big clump of grass. When he puts the clump on my cast, it's like a little yard growing out of me. "I better go." Before he stands up, he puts Tiger on my lap.

"Wait! How do you know they'll be okay?"

If my mom yelled for me like that I'd be running, but Gordy's just standing there slapping grass off his pants, like he isn't scared at all. "Well, they aren't all caged up anymore, are they? They can do anything now, they're free."

On his way home, Gordy grabs an apple off the ground. I'm sure that apple has a wormhole in it but he takes a bite out of it anyway. Without even looking.

"Don't you let that Tiger get you," I whisper to Thunder, but I'm only joking. I can already tell they're going to get along fine.

Acknowledgments

So many people to thank:

Susan Rich, you first—for the huge gift of believing in my writing, and for so brilliantly and lovingly editing this book. (Rachel Gorenstein, I owe you a thousand lunches for the introduction.)

Charlotte Sheedy, a better agent than I could have ever dreamed up, thank you for your love and support—and for suggesting that I turn one of my short stories into a middle grade novel. This book would never have come into being without you.

Tom Spanbauer, my beloved writing teacher, I'm not exaggerating when I say that you changed my life.

I'd be lost in space without my writing community: Elizabeth Scott, Robert Hill, Dian Greenwood, Gigi Little, Steve Arnt, Laura Stanfill, Margaret Malone, Sara Guest, Diane Ponti, Michael Sage Ricci, David Ciminello, Joe Rogers, Wes Griffith, Colin Farstad, Kevin Meyer, Mary Wharff, Liz Fischer Greenhill, Domi Shoemaker, Davis Slater, Stephen O'Donnell, Liz Prato, so many others.

Huge thanks to my middle school advisors: Meredith Bolls, Harper Gladysz, Sage Reagan, Natalie Lauritsen, Zora Berkeley, Milena Kelsey, Rachael Berkeley, Liz Kobs.

My friends/safety net: Alison Apotheker, Fontaine Roberson, Robyn Tenenbaum, Marlene Paul, Julie Gedrose, Lella Poppa.

Leo and Tucky, most wonderful boys *on earth*, thank you for your patience, editorial advice, humor, and love.

And Jelly, you above all—for your steady love, support, and friendship—and for saying so many years ago, "Maybe you should be a writer."